MW01282161

THE SWITHERBY PILGRIMS

Also by Eleanor Spence

Patterson's Track
The Summer in Between
Lillipilly Hill
The Green Laurel
The Year of the Currawong
Jamberoo Road (Sequel to *The Switherby Pilgrims*)
Time to Go Home
The Nothing-Place
The October Child
The Seventh Pebble
The Left Overs
Me and Jeshua

The
Switherby Pilgrims
A Tale of the Australian Bush

Eleanor Spence

BETHLEHEM BOOKS · IGNATIUS PRESS
BATHGATE, ND   SAN FRANCISCO

© 1967 Eleanor Spence

Cover art © 2005 Ezra Tucker
Cover design by Theodore Schluenderfritz
Inside decorations by Roseanne Sharpe

First Bethlehem Books Printing April 2005

All rights reserved

ISBN 1-883937-99-7
Library of Congress Catalog Number: 2005921336

Bethlehem Books • Ignatius Press
10194 Garfield St. South
Bathgate, North Dakota 58216
www.bethlehembooks.com
800 757 6831

Printed in the United States on acid-free paper

Kingery Printing Company
2916 Marshall Ave.
Mattoon, Il 61938
February 2021 Printing

Job # 190149

Author's Note

All characters in this story are fictitious, with the exception of Thomas Rose of Appin, and Dr. Halloran of the Sydney (Free) Grammar School. Brief mention is also made of John Macarthur and Governor Ralph Darling. For information on these people, on the historical background generally, and on the Illawarra District particularly, I am indebted to the *Journals and Proceedings* of the Royal Australian Historical Society.

E.S.

Publisher's Note

British spellings in the original text have been changed for the sake of our predominately American readership.

Contents

THE SWITHERBY PILGRIMS

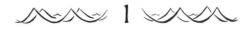

Miss Braithwaite Counts Her Burdens

HER PROPER NAME was Miss Arabella Jane Braithwaite, and so she might always have been known had it not been for an outbreak of typhus in her home village of Switherby, early in March, ten years after the Battle of Waterloo.

In Switherby, Waterloo was long since forgotten; indeed, it had not been greatly remarked even at the time it was fought. Switherby had then been but a small village, tucked away behind a ridge just north of the center of England. It was the tiny unhurried heart of a farming district where nothing seemed to have altered greatly since Roundheads and Cavaliers fought across the fields. The farmers brought their produce to Switherby for sale, and the farmers' wives their woven shawls and pats of butter and crocks of cheese, and their leisurely gossip to regale in the little market-square beside the Saxon church. Two of Switherby's sons had died at Waterloo, and young Oliver Brown had lost a leg and most of his health, but after a week or two the talk in Switherby was once again mostly of the seasons and the spinning, the betrothals and the babies.

Miss Arabella's father had been the Vicar in those days, preaching to a sleepy sun-reddened or wind-chapped congregation in the squat stone church by the market-place, the church of St. Matthew the Lower. It was called thus to distinguish it from the other St. Matthew's, a mile away up on the ridge among the fields. When Miss Arabella's brother Hugh succeeded his father as Vicar, six years after Waterloo, St. Matthew's the Higher was no longer out in the country, but rather linked with Switherby by a ragged chain of low brick cottages and a rough well-trodden road. Life was changing at last, and as the farmers' pastures were gradually enclosed, and new steam-powered factories rose bleakly along the valley, more and more bewildered country-folk moved in to make Switherby a larger and larger village, until it could almost be called a small town.

"And much good that has done us," remarked the Reverend Hugh sadly. "What shall I do for peoples' souls when their bodies are not getting enough food?"

"We must see to the food first," answered his practical sister.

Certainly she did her best, for whatever Miss Arabella did she tried to do thoroughly. No one was ever turned away hungry from the vicarage door, even if it meant that the vicar's sister had to turn to and help the overworked cook, or share out the roast-beef prepared for their own dinner. But Miss Arabella had not the means to clothe the unemployed in winter, or to pay their overdue rent or give them warm beds. Nor could she rescue all the babies and small children who succumbed to every ailment known to man, because lack of good food sapped their resistance.

"I can still help the older children," she said, refusing to admit defeat. "I shall start a school."

The old shabby vicarage had space enough for several classes, but as Miss Arabella expected to be the only teacher, she prepared only one room, the back parlor which opened on to an overgrown rose-garden. She dragged downstairs all the nursery furniture and some wobbly wooden chairs which she found in the attic, stocked up on slates and pencils and samplers, and asked her brother to broadcast news of her school from the pulpit.

"No fees charged, of course," she added. "And I shall take both boys and girls from four years old."

In theory, it seemed promising. Switherby boasted one grammar-school and a small private establishment for young ladies, but both of these required fees, and Miss Arabella was hoping to attract the sons and daughters of the poorer folk. She had plenty of faith in her own ability to instruct them; she had been educated along with her brother, first by a governess and then by a tutor, and had had the freedom of the vicarage's ample untidy library. All she needed was a supply of pupils.

A week passed, however, and the number had not exceeded eight. In the second week two more appeared, but three others left. It continued thus throughout a term, with the average enrollment standing at seven.

"There are *dozens* of children in Switherby who should be at school," sighed Miss Arabella. "Why don't they come?"

"Why don't their fathers and mothers come to church any more?" asked the Vicar gloomily. "I can tell you why—it's because they work so hard on all the other days that they're too tired to go anywhere on Sundays. Or they haven't any clothes fit to wear. And the children work, too—that's why they don't come to your school. Even at eight or nine the children can earn a few shillings a week in the factories.

In the old days they worked, too, but then it was clean work on the farms, with plenty to eat and a good night's rest."

"We talk too much of the old days," objected Miss Arabella. "It is here and now that we must help."

For another four years she struggled along with her tiny school, coaxing and scolding and praising her pupils while she forced the rudiments of education into their often weary heads. It was a discouraging business. Her few promising charges usually left after one or two terms, when their parents found employment for them, or decided to move on to one of the larger towns. Those who might have won scholarships to the grammar-school were not permitted to go because their fathers could no longer support them in what was generally considered idleness. Only a very small measure of success came to Miss Arabella, from two sources. One was from the family of Oliver Brown, the Waterloo veteran now deceased. His widow was a valiant little woman who did every manner of work in and around Switherby in order that her three children, and in particular the older boy, Francis, should have a sound education and consequently secure employment. The children showed every sign of fulfilling their mother's prodigious ambition, and were Miss Arabella's pride.

The second source of satisfaction had literally appeared on the vicarage doorstep, a minute tattered wailing bundle abandoned by its unknown mother one vicious midwinter night. The mother had certainly shown some foresight, for had the baby been left at the door of the district workhouse its chances of healthy survival would have been greatly diminished. As it was, Miss Arabella refused steadfastly to turn the child over to the local authorities—who in any case had their hands more than full—and added its exacting care to her long list of parish and domestic duties. The child was duly christened Sarah Louisa, and in time began toddling about the schoolroom during lessons, being petted and admired by the older girls, who called her Sally-Lou. Miss Arabella secretly believed that her foundling was of gypsy stock, so dark-eyed and black of hair was she, but if Miss Arabella had anything to say in the matter, Sally-Lou would undoubtedly grow up a well-educated and well-spoken young English lady.

And so it might have been. But the typhus epidemic struck Switherby, and Miss Arabella's plans underwent a drastic change.

Epidemics of various kinds had occurred many times before, of course, and everyone accepted them as inevitable strokes of fate. In the old days, however, when the farms were scattered and the village small, illnesses did not spread so far and so fast. With Switherby now overcrowded and standards of hygiene at their lowest, with whole families living and sleeping in one damp un-ventilated room, and only one harassed doctor in the entire town, the typhus raged like a fire out of control.

At the vicarage, Miss Arabella and her brother fought it grimly throughout that dreary spring, risking their own lives to save at least the children of the worst-affected families. When Oliver Brown's widow became ill with the disease, Miss Arabella kept the three children at the vicarage, along with several other pupils whose own parents were unable to look after them. Her greatest fear was for Sally-Lou, now an active prancing four-year-old, but apparently one heritage the child had acquired from her vanished forebears was a remarkable constitution, for she survived the epidemic untouched.

Spring came slowly to Switherby, covering the vicarage elms with drifts of green, and setting the churchyard aglow with daffodils. More and more people began to venture forth again into market-place and factory, and on Sundays the church was no longer three-fourths empty—only half-vacant, as before the epidemic. Gladly, Miss Arabella and the cook threw open the windows and doors to admit the warming sun, and the schoolroom was put in order for its returning pupils.

But some of the vacancies in Switherby were permanent. Miss Arabella's face grew sad and thoughtful as she talked with her brother after Evensong one beautiful day in June. They sat in the study facing the church, where the sunlight lingered on golden-brown stone and jewelled glass.

"I fear Mrs. Brown had no chance at all, poor soul," said the Reverend Hugh, still tired and pale from those hectic weeks. "She was quite worn out even before she took ill. And that other widow, poor Mrs. Crosley the dressmaker— she slaved to keep the little girl."

"Selina—her mother never let her come to school for fear of her catching an illness," observed Miss Arabella. "Yet the child came through this quite safely, I believe. Hugh, how many new orphans are there in our parish?"

"Apart from the Browns and Selina Crosley, and those two little Scots fellows you once had in your school—let me see, there are the Gracechurch children. Their father is living, but he's precious little use to them, I'm afraid. Always drunk, and ill-treating that poor boy. If you count them, that makes nine. Several others have already gone to the work-house."

Miss Arabella stared fixedly at a brilliant forsythia bloom-ing by the churchyard wall. She was seeing, not the golden blossoms, but the great grey bulk of the Bingleton work-house, ten miles away.

"And the Browns will go, too?"

Her brother sighed.

"Where else can they go? And you know, Arabella, the present head of the work-house is a most humane man—the children are never badly used there."

"Perhaps not," agreed Miss Arabella. "They are simply put out to work for twelve hours a day, and sent home to sleep in a huge bare room with absolutely nothing to call their own. Mrs. Brown was always so sure that Francis at least would make his mark in the world, and grow up to keep his sister and brother in comfort. Francis will be fortunate now if he rises to be overseer in the hardware factory."

The Reverend Hugh gazed at his sister in pity and per-plexity.

"My dear, all this is perfectly true, and regrettable, but try as we might, we cannot put right all the wrongs of the world, or even of Switherby."

Miss Arabella studied the forsythia for several more min-utes, and when she spoke again she seemed to have changed the subject completely—although her brother, knowing her so well, remained a little wary.

"Now that the worst of the epidemic is over," said Miss Arabella, "I suppose you will go on with your plans to be married in the summer?"

"If Charlotte is willing," answered the Vicar cautiously.

He had been betrothed for some months to the daughter of a neighboring minister in Bingleton, and his sister had taken the news very calmly at the time. She had, indeed, been delighted at his choice of a wife, for Charlotte was both cheerful and conscientious, and would make an excellent mistress of the vicarage.

"I hope you won't be inconvenienced if some of these children remain at the vicarage for a few weeks," Arabella continued.

"Of course not, Bella. You know, both Charlotte and I should be only too pleased to have you here indefinitely, and goodness knows, there's enough room for a dozen children, if that's what you want. But," he added shrewdly, "that's *not* what you want, is it?"

Miss Arabella at last removed her gaze from the window, and looked at her brother squarely. She was a small, slight lady, with mouse-colored hair and an indifferent complexion unflattered by her choice of grey or lilac as dress-materials, but her eyes were fine and commanding, and reminded the Reverend Hugh that his sister had been a determined and dominating character since their nursery days.

"You are quite right, Hugh—I have other plans. You will no doubt call them outrageous, but my mind is made up. These children must have a new start in life, and a chance to do something worthwhile with their lives. So I am going to take them away."

"You mean to another village? I understand conditions are bad almost everywhere just now—"

"Exactly. So I intend to take them to New South Wales."

Had she named the moon or the planet Venus as her destination, her brother would hardly have been more astonished. He considered himself a rather well-traveled clergyman, having been once to Scotland, twice to Wales, and at least half a dozen times to London. He even hoped to visit the Continent one day. But his sister had led the sheltered life customary to one of her class, and as far as he could recall, the farthest point of her travels had been Harrogate. In his agitation he began to pace up and down the study, hands clenched behind his clerical coat-tails.

"Arabella, you must be joking. Why, you've never been even to London! Have you any idea what New South Wales is like?"

"No," said his sister calmly. "Have you?"

"Only a faint idea, but hardly an attractive one. A penal settlement, a refuge for vagabonds and freed ruffians and vicious speculators. They even arrested their own Governor."

"That was over ten years ago, Hugh. I have been reading the newspapers very carefully. It seems that one may make application for a free passage and a grant of land in the colony. It is a huge country, I believe. And there are many perfectly respectable families out there now. Don't you remember that the Appletons from Saffron Towers all emigrated to New South Wales last summer?"

"The Appletons?" repeated the Reverend Hugh in a dazed way. "But, Bella—they had money, influence, any number of servants and household goods. What shall *you* have?"

Miss Arabella sat up very straight.

"More than you realize. I have courage and a pair of hands and a head as good as any man's—and I shall also take Father's endowment."

Still bewildered, not knowing whether to mock or admire his sister's foolhardiness, the Vicar came to the study table and lit the lamps. Automatically, Miss Arabella rose to draw the curtains.

"The money Father left me is mine to invest as I please," she went on imperturbably. "I am choosing to invest it in these unfortunate children."

"It is not a great amount, Bella. Until some of the children can be employed, you must clothe and feed them from your own resources. What if you fail?"

"That is unlikely. Should it happen, however, they will be no worse off than they are here. At least out there they will have clean air to breathe."

Absently, the Vicar drew out his watch and began to wind it.

"I don't know what to think—"

"You are right—it is time for bed, and thoughts can wait until the morning. I must be up early, for I have letters to write. Good-night, Hugh."

***

Letter-writing was luckily no hardship to Miss Arabella. Indeed, she revelled in it, even with Sally-Lou tugging at her skirts and wanting to play with the pen. Before midday the letters had been written and dispatched, one to the Under-Secretary for the Colonies, one for the local Magistrate, and one to distant Mrs. Maria Appleton in New South Wales.

This first important step having been taken, Miss Arabella did not sit back to await results. She still had her school to run, her increased household to see to, and her church duties were not neglected. Her energy, always considerable, seemed to have reached a new remarkable level, and the poor Vicar often felt as if a whirlwind had entered his house. He would come in after Matins to find the hall littered with cast-off clothing that Miss Arabella had begged from the more wealthy parishioners, and enter the schoolroom only to find the children engaged in reciting details of colonial geography and economics. Even little Sally-Lou prattled of Sydney Town and the big ship that would take her there.

"Aren't you afraid of disappointing them?" asked the Vicar. "After all, nothing has been settled."

"These matters take time," said Miss Arabella serenely. "Have you approached that Gracechurch man yet?"

"He can't be found. The children are with a neighbor, awaiting removal to the work-house. But I spoke to Angus MacBain, and he is quite willing for his two nephews to be placed in your care."

"Good," said Miss Arabella with satisfaction. "Then apart from the Gracechurches, there is only the Crosley child to be added to our list. I shall see about that this afternoon."

The parish register gave the Crosleys' address as Canary Lane, and Miss Arabella could only hope that the child would still be there. So overcrowded was the work-house that many paupers and orphans had to be placed on a grim kind of waiting-list, and in the interim many disappeared in ways that could merely be shudderingly surmised.

Canary Lane was half-way up the ridge between the two St. Matthews, a grimy slit of an alley enclosed by sooty blank walls. The hardware factory was but a stone's-throw away, and a steam laundry close by in another direction. It was of course familiar enough to Miss Arabella, yet she still sighed to remember Canary Lane as it once was, a pretty little by-way leading to the open country.

Closer inspection of the wall revealed brick archways over scuffed wooden doors, and on one of these was a square of cardboard in a metal frame.

" 'Ladies' Gowns and Millinery—Mrs. Crosley'," read Miss Arabella. "But someone has crossed out 'Mrs.' and written 'Miss' instead. Oh, the poor child!"

More determined than ever that Selina must be rescued, Miss Arabella knocked loudly at the door. It was opened very quickly indeed—no doubt customers were so few and far between that they must be admitted without delay.

"Was it gowns or hats you wanted?" asked a hopeful and undeniably childish voice from the dank gloom within.

"Neither. I'm from the vicarage. May I come in?"

Remarkable strength would have been needed to resist Miss Arabella in her most purposeful mood, and the child did not attempt to stop her visitor's entry into the one tiny cluttered room that was the dressmaker's shop. Two inadequate candles burnt fitfully on a bench, perilously close to remnants of muslin and lawn; a few half-finished bonnets graced a shelf, and a work-basket stood on the floor, its contents overflowing on to a worn rug. The only air in the room came from the door, which Miss Arabella left ajar.

"You must be Selina Crosley?"

The child nodded. Her white pointed face was wary enough, but the usual sullen fear of destitution was absent. Whatever this child lacked, it was not spirit. She was remarkably clean, too, and her muslin frock, though faded and darned, was well made. Her features were fine and pleasing, her long soft hair a silvery color where the light touched it.

"Do you mind if I leave the door open?" Miss Arabella went on. "It's really such a lovely summer day. Don't let me interrupt if you're busy."

She had not intended any sarcasm, but the girl gave her a quick suspicious glance.

"I'm not busy. People don't come any more. They think I'm too young, but I'm good at sewing."

Her voice was almost too refined, Miss Arabella thought. She could remember vaguely hearing some gossip about the late Mrs. Crosley, who was supposed to have married above her station and been deserted when Selina was a baby. Perhaps it had been true, after all.

"How old are you, Selina?"

"Eleven. How do you know my name?"

Miss Arabella had not expected such alertness. Accustomed though she was to dealing firmly and sensibly with children, she felt instinctively that Selina needed to be carefully handled if she was to be added to the emigration list. And added she must be— how long could the child exist like this, like a little fox run to earth and slowly starving?

"Your mother belonged to our parish. I have taken some other children to the vicarage to live—ones without parents, you know—and the Vicar has been anxious about you."

"I'm all right," declared Selina. "I don't need charity."

"Oh, it's not charity, exactly," said Miss Arabella hurriedly. "You see, I'm planning to take some children out to New South Wales, where they will learn to do useful work in a new country."

"Where's that?" asked Selina. "Is it far?"

"Very far. I won't pretend that it will be an easy life, but we shall all be together, and help each other. And perhaps you will learn to be a first-class dressmaker there—I understand, dressmakers are in demand."

Again came that swift suspicious glance.

"And what if I don't want to go?"

"Are there any relatives here who would look after you? I thought not. Sooner or later, Selina, you would be taken to the work-house. I'm not trying to frighten you, you understand—it is for you to decide."

Selina stood in the middle of the dreary little room, gazing at the few possessions her mother had left her, and for a moment the anguish and uncertainty of the child that she really was, displaced the veneer of the independent genteel young lady she had tried to be. Tactfully, Miss Arabella turned towards the door.

"Mrs. Jones upstairs has been letting me eat with them," Selina admitted. "But there's talk of them going away soon. Shall I come to the vicarage when they leave?"

"Come any time. Bring whatever clothes and belongings you want—we may have to embark at quite short notice."

And as she made her way homewards past the factory and along the mean streets, Miss Arabella sincerely hoped, for the sake of her charges, that the notice would be short indeed.

 2

A Stir in the Schoolroom

"MISSABELLA, IT'S MY turn to watch for the post today, isn't it? Cassie did it yesterday."

Paul Brown stood hopefully before the schoolroom desk, balancing on the tips of his toes, for the desk was very high and Paul somewhat short, even allowing for the fact that he was only eight years old. He was dressed as usual in a suit that his brother Francis had outgrown, and despite generous tucks here and there, the trousers still reached the heels of his shoes, and the sleeves of his blouse were draggled at the cuffs through being too close to his plate at mealtimes. His round blue eyes gazed upwards with their habitual solemn anxiety at the person whom he now regarded as mother, father and schoolteacher all merged into one.

"You are quite right, Paul. You may take your slate and sit near the window, and go on with the words you were learning yesterday. It is a little early for the postman yet."

Nevertheless, her own gaze was not infrequently directed outdoors as she listened to Cassandra Brown reading in French. Normally this accomplishment of Cassie's was a source of considerable pleasure to Miss Arabella, for the child had begun to learn the language only a few weeks

15

previously, at her own request. It would hardly be necessary for a girl like Cassie to be fluent in French, particularly in the Colonies, but she learnt so quickly and so eagerly that teaching her any subject was a delight. And in any case, thought Miss Arabella in unwonted gloom, she might never reach New South Wales, and would stay on at the vicarage as a teaching assistant.

"Martha, come and write the date on the board, please. Your very best handwriting."

Martha Gracechurch approached nervously and began to write, her tongue thrust out and her snub nose screwed up with the intensity of her effort. Learning certainly did not come easily to Martha, who had been almost illiterate before her arrival at the vicarage in the spring. Had Cassie not whispered the day's date to her from behind her French primer, Martha would indeed have been lost.

"Now read it aloud, please."

"The twenty-third of August, eighteen-'undred-an'-twenty-five", Martha pronounced laboriously.

"Again, if you please. Let me hear 'h' and 'd'."

The lessons continued. The day was one of rare clarity and brilliance, a fine summer day that made one think of long walks in the country and solid meals at wayside inns, or of journeys to the sea. Miss Arabella sighed a little, for the sea was beginning to seem impossibly distant, and New South Wales as remote as the moon. Three months had passed since she had written her letters, and to two of them no reply had come. The third had brought a brief response from the local Magistrate—who was also the Switherby squire and Master of the Bingleton Hunt—agreeing to supply a testimonial on her behalf to the Colonial Secretary. She and the children had gone on hoping, but very soon she must make some alternative plan for the children's future. The Vicar was to be married in a week or two, and his bride could hardly be expected to have her new home transformed into a sort of private orphanage. Besides, funds were running low . . .

"Please, Missabella, I've finished me pot-hooks. What shall I do now?"

It was the other Gracechurch twin, Marianne, an even less promising scholar than Martha. Nature had intended the Gracechurch girls to be round and rosy and placid, but nature had failed to provide the right sort of nourishment, so that the twins' flesh hung loose on their large frames, and their short-sighted eyes were dulled by years of struggle against hunger and want and a drunken, bad-tempered father. Fortunately for his children, Josiah Gracechurch had disappeared completely after the death of his wife, and Miss Arabella had had no difficulty in assuming the guardianship of the ten-year-old twins and their younger brother.

"Perhaps some sewing would be best, Marianne. You like that, don't you? Martha, you may take out your sampler also. What is it, Paul?"

Miss Arabella—now "Missabella" to all her pupils— would no longer allow herself to become excited over the arrival of the post, but to the children it was the big event of the day, even more important than their regular walk across the market-square to the public gardens. Even studious Cassie, and her brother Francis who was almost thirteen, glanced eagerly towards the window as Paul cried the news of the postman's approach.

In a few moments the cook was at the schoolroom door.

"Please, Miss, Postie has something he has to give to you personal."

"Francis, look after the children," said Missabella. She rose with slow dignity, smoothing her lilac skirts and adjusting her coil of hair as if in readiness for a portentous meeting. Once away from the schoolroom, however, she moved at a pace very lively for a spinster of thirty-eight.

Francis shut the schoolroom door and took his place at the high desk. He was nearly as tall as Missabella, and as thin, and his watchful expression was that of a much older lad. For five years he had tried hard to be the man of the Brown household, and that had given him little enough time to be a child.

"We must all get on with our work," he announced. "Even you, Sally-Lou. Where's your pencil?"

Sally-Lou was in her usual position on the floor beside the desk, where Missabella could watch her continuously. Like Marianne, Sally-Lou should have been practicing pothooks, but her five-year-old yearning for activity had driven her instead to try a somersault or two while Missabella was out of the room.

"Can't find it," she said, in a voice muffled by her petticoats.

"Let her play," said Cassie indulgently. "She's too little for school."

"I wish I could play, too," Paul protested. "I don't feel like spelling any more."

"Do you suppose it really *is* the letter this time?" asked Cassie. "It's no good pretending to be a school-teacher, Francis—you know you're just as interested as we are."

"If it's the right letter, shall we be going to New South Wales tomorrow?" asked Martha, staring at the schoolroom globe whose arrangements of islands and continents she was never able to remember. Like all the other children, she had not been any further than Bingleton.

"Not *tomorrow*," Francis objected. "We have to go to London first."

He gave up his attempt to stop the chatter, and turned to study the globe himself. New South Wales, he reflected, was just half a world away from Switherby—about five months' sailing time, or so Miss Arabella had said. Five months! That was the interval which had elapsed since the death of his mother, and already it seemed remote. Francis was a conscientious boy, who strove hard to obey the remembered injunctions of his parents, but it was becoming increasingly difficult to keep them in the forefront of his mind. He liked Missabella's little school, and knew only too well how lucky he was to be still free from the shadow of the factory or the workshop at the advanced age of twelve. He fully intended to study as much as he could, and to obtain the gentlemanly position of articled clerk that his mother had wished for him. And yet—Francis had his own secret, absurd ambition, not even known to Cassie, and it was because of this that he was so desperately interested in Missabella's emigration scheme. He had been taught not to hope too much, but nothing could prevent his dreaming.

"Missabella is a long time coming," said Cassie restlessly. She pushed the heavy auburn hair away from her forehead and bent once more over her book. If only little pictures of sailing-ships and coaches would stop dancing in her head!

"Had I best go and see where Robin is?" asked Marianne, who disliked doing anything on her own initiative. "He might be bothering Cook."

"I'll go," offered Cassie eagerly, and dashed from the room before Francis could stop her. She just *had* to know what was happening, and not to Robin Gracechurch, either. She was fond enough of Robin—they all were, little simpleton that he was— but he was far too docile to be in any trouble, and it was the study, not the kitchen, that she wanted to investigate. So she slipped past the cook's domain and through the back door, into the shrubbery between the side wall of the vicarage and the churchyard. The sunlight crept through the branches of lilac and laburnum, and the earth smelt rich and warm as Cassie crouched below the study window. Could there be any news but good news on such a generous day?

The Vicar was there, speaking now in the deep resonant voice that always made Cassie think of the cool stone cavern of the church, and of the gleaming windows depicting scenes from Revelations. She listened more closely now than she usually did during his sermons, which tended to wander into abstract and scholarly by-ways.

"I only wish it were more definite, Bella," the Vicar was saying. "You won't know until you reach the Colony just where or of what value your grant will be. It could be miles from civilization, and then how ever will you manage with all those children?"

"That's a bridge we don't have to cross yet," Missabella replied, on an unmistakable note of triumph. "Our first and most important bridge *has* been crossed, and that is getting permission to sail. I must say I was rather wondering whether perhaps the Colonial Secretary had decided, one middle-aged woman, with ten orphans, might be an unsuitable emigrant."

"I could have agreed with him," said the Vicar gloomily. "I do wish you would reconsider, Bella."

"It's far too late now. Our passages are reserved, and we have only six weeks in which to make our preparations. So we must get to work at once."

Cassie waited no longer. She crawled back through the shrubbery as rapidly as the long trailing skirts of her gown permitted— fortunately it was a drab brown and would not show the dirt— and raced for the schoolroom. Her voice had to be kept to a whisper, but it was the most dramatic and piercing whisper possible.

"It's happened! It really has! We're leaving in six weeks!"

"You've been listening at doors again," said Francis reprovingly, and then added at once: "What sort of ship will it be?"

"I knew the letter would come today, because it was my turn to watch," said Paul, who liked to have his own small private triumphs. "I even saw the letter in the postman's hand."

"Shall I be sea-sick?" enquired Sally-Lou. "Will there be sea-serpents?"

"Oh dear!" sighed Martha. "Now it's happened, I think I like Switherby best. Don't you, Marianne?"

"If it's the vicarage you mean, then I do," agreed her sister. "But if Missabella goes, we have to go too, even if there's black men."

"There's one thing," meditated Cassie. "Missabella said she would have ten orphans with her, and there are only seven of us here, counting Sally-Lou. I wonder who the others are?"

"More boys, I hope," said Francis. "You have to have boys on a farm, to carry water and chop wood and plow up the fields."

"We don't know for sure that it will be a farm," Cassie pointed out. "Anyway, all the girls will be able to work hard, except Sally-Lou."

The youngest orphan was about to make a vigorous objection to this statement, when the door opened and Missabella reappeared. Although normally she clung to the belief that it was undignified to show too much emotion of any kind, Missabella could not on this occasion keep all the light from her eyes nor completely control the upward quirk of her mouth. Instinctively, the older children assumed straight faces and pretended to know nothing of the news, while Sally-Lou and Paul were restrained by Cassie and Francis respectively.

Missabella took her place behind the desk and tapped it loudly with her pointer. It was a brisk tapping, like the rat-tat-tat of a military drum.

"Children," said Missabella, "we have been officially informed that we may proceed to New South Wales, embarking on the fifth of October."

The children felt free to cheer. Cook and Robin came from the kitchen to see what was happening, and the Vicar, passing down the hall, could not help smiling at the sight of so many bright and excited faces.

"In honor of the occasion," went on Missabella, "we shall declare a half-holiday and take our tea to Saffron Woods. Having enjoyed our holiday, we must then settle down to some hard work to be ready for our departure. What is it, Francis?"

"You forgot to tell us the name of the ship, Ma'am," said Francis, respectfully but firmly.

"Let me see," said Missabella, taking out her letter. "Yes, it's the *Medway Queen*, and her home port is Gravesend. I don't have any more information than that about the ship herself."

"Will it be a sailing-ship, then?" asked Martha, who had

seen no craft larger than the canal-barges.

"What else *could it* be?" demanded Cassie impatiently. She often found the twins' slowness highly exasperating, though she was gentle enough with their much more retarded younger brother.

"It just could be one of those new paddle-steamers," Francis pointed out. "But I don't think they could go as far as New South Wales."

"What's a paddle-steamer?" asked Cassie, ever on the alert for fresh information.

"I saw a picture of one in the *Switherby Gazette*—I'll try and draw it for you."

Paul, who had returned to his seat of honor at the window, now had his second triumph of the morning.

"Please, Missabella, there's someone at the door—a lady. At least, it *might* be a lady," added Paul, his nose pressed to the pane.

"Ladies don't come to backdoors," said Missabella. "Cassie, go and see what she wants, please."

Sadly overcrowded though Missabella's curriculum was, she had tried to find a place in it for deportment, for the benefit of the girls. The twins were not built for grace, and Sally-Lou was far too young to understand the social value of a straight back and a dignified bearing, so Missabella hoped that Cassie might once again prove to be the ablest pupil. Here, however, she had been disappointed. Cassie at eleven should have been giving some thought to her manners and her dress, but she was not interested in these at all. She moved like a boy, with long strides and continual haste; her thick auburn hair straggled over her shoulders, and always appeared in need of brushing. Invited to choose garments for herself from the charity collection, she took whatever came first to hand, and gave no heed to their suitability in relation to her fair and somewhat freckled complexion. Missabella persevered, but she often worried in secret over this outspoken determined child who had so much intelligence, and so little of that highly desirable feminine quality—charm.

Thus it was that when Cassie opened the vicarage backdoor on that eventful morning, she was confronted with a creature who was almost her exact opposite. Selina Crosley had finally been obliged to seek the refuge Missabella had offered, and there she stood, in the very best dress her mother had lovingly made the previous summer, a pink muslin creation complete with matching bonnet and imitation-lace mittens. How was Cassie to know that Selina's shiny black shoes were the only ones she had, and small to the point of pinching her toes?

Cassie forgot the few manners she had, and simply stared. Selina, already nervous and apprehensive, tried to hide her embarrassment by assuming her most refined accents.

"Is the lady of the vicarage at home?"

"If you mean Miss Arabella Braithwaite, then she is," answered Cassie, as abruptly as she dared.

"She asked me to come," said Selina. I'm Miss Crosley."

At this moment Robin wandered into the hall, for being almost unteachable by ordinary schoolroom standards, he had the freedom of the vicarage and the grounds, provided someone kept an eye on him. He was nine years old, but even smaller than Paul Brown, and an early accident—for which Josiah Gracechurch was probably responsible—had left him with a shortened left leg and a dragging gait. Robin was a cheerful, docile little fellow, devoted to his sisters and to Missabella; however, his awkward stammering speech and unprepossessing appearance were certainly not designed to reassure a stranger. As he spoke and gesticulated to Cassie, Selina backed away.

"It's all right—it's only Robin," said Cassie impatiently. "You'd better come in."

Robin was fascinated by the color of Selina's dress, and trod close on her heels as Cassie led the way to the schoolroom. To poor Selina, the sad, damp little room in Canary Lane had begun to seem a delightful refuge, and she wished she had never left it, although yesterday the family upstairs had departed, leaving Selina as alone as any orphaned child in all England.

Cassie marched into the schoolroom with the announcement: "This is Miss Crosley, Ma'am," and went back to her seat, pretending thereafter to ignore the visitor's presence altogether. There was some sort of inborn elegance about Selina that caused Cassie an inward and unaccustomed discomfort.

But there was no lack of enthusiasm in Missabella's welcome.

"Selina, my dear! We have been hoping you would come. This is just the right day, too. Take off your bonnet and sit down there beside Marianne, while I explain what has happened."

Selina could only obey. Carefully she untied her bonnet strings and laid the dainty headgear on the bench beside her. The sight of its wide, stiff brim, and the posy of artificial daisies that adorned it, brought back the memory of her mother, sitting night after night at her work-table, her eyes straining in the dim light. Selina would be in her half of the bed in the corner of the room, listening, sleepy but enthralled, to her mother's stories of her girlhood, when she was a dainty little seamstress being wooed by the most handsome officer of the regiment stationed near by.

"His father owned a real castle up in Northumberland, and one day, so Captain Crosley said, he would take me there to live, and I should be the grandest lady in the district, giving balls for all the gentry. But we were wed quietly, because of the fighting in France and thereabouts, and not long afterwards he went off with his regiment."

"And was he killed in battle?" Selina would ask.

"He must have been, for he never came back. He would not have forgotten us, I'm sure."

"Then why don't you go and see his father and mother in the castle?"

But her mother would only peer more closely at her sewing, and shake her head.

"It's a long way, and I never knew quite where this castle was. I want you to remember, though, that you had a fine gentleman for a father, and you must always try to act like a lady."

Missabella was saying something about New South Wales, but Selina hardly heard her. She had come to the vicarage simply because there was nowhere else to go, and she did recall vaguely that Missabella had spoken of emigrating; to Selina it was a completely unreal and incomprehensible notion. Just now she was furtively examining the other occupants of the schoolroom, more than a little dismayed by their number and by their collective appearance. They *looked* like charity children—was she, Selina Crosley, to become like them, dressed in obviously cast-off clothing?

She caught the glance of the oldest boy, who was smiling at her over a Latin grammar. He had a rather pleasant face, and kind dark eyes, but his hair was of the same auburn shade as that of the alarming girl who had met Selina at the backdoor. Could he be her brother? And what was the Vicar's sister saying now?

"Tomorrow, instead of doing ordinary lessons, we shall write out notices to display in the church porch, asking for donations of blankets and provisions. My friend, Mrs. Appleton, has written to me from New South Wales, and she tells me that although the climate is mild, the winter nights are cold, and the houses very drafty. So we shall need more warm clothing, also."

Missabella did not add that the general tone of Mrs. Appleton's letter had been far from encouraging. Sydney Town, she claimed, was a drab and uncivilized place, and out in the country one was constantly beset by every kind of annoyance, ranging from insect bites to floods. And yet the Appletons might reasonably be expected to have far more creature comforts than Missabella and her orphans could hope for. In her present optimistic mood, however, Missabella decided that Mrs. Appleton was naturally of a gloomy and discontented disposition.

Meanwhile, Selina was aghast at the prospect of having to beg for the necessities of life. Hurriedly she stood up.

"But Ma'am, I already have warm clothes, and blankets, too. A boy from Canary Lane is bringing everything up this afternoon."

Cassie scowled, and the Gracechurch twins were open-mouthed at the thought of such wealth. When they had arrived at the vicarage, they had possessed only the few garments they wore, and Robin had not even owned a pair of shoes.

"Then you are fortunate, Selina," said Missabella calmly.

"But I must ask you to help with the notices, all the same. I shall send one to the *Gazette,* and perhaps Mrs. Simkins will put one in her shop. We shall need at least three, and only you and Francis and Cassie can write."

"How can you write when you've never been to school?" demanded Cassie afterwards, as she helped clear away the dinner dishes. Selina's dainty manners at table had merely heightened Cassie's mistrust.

"My mother taught me," replied Selina. "And my father taught *her.* He was a cavalry officer."

"Our father was wounded at Waterloo," put in Paul eagerly. "He had only one leg. Was your father at Waterloo?"

Selina hesitated, and sharp-eyed Cassie pounced.

"Where is he now?"

"He was killed when his horse bolted," said Selina, in an unwonted and desperate flight of imagination. "I don't remember, because I was a baby then."

Paul and Francis were impressed and suitably sympathetic, but Cassie remained sceptical. In the days that followed, she and Selina avoided each other by mutual consent, for they seemed to have absolutely nothing in common. As Selina grew more accustomed to her new mode of life, she learned to seek out the jobs most agreeable to her, like sorting linen and helping with the sewing. She had a natural talent with her needle, and scored a small triumph by designing a simple white silk tunic for Sally-Lou, who had been selected to strew rose-petals before the bride and groom at the Vicar's wedding.

"I think that's a silly sort of dress," remarked Cassie, as a highly delighted Sally-Lou paraded around the schoolroom in her finery. "Is it supposed to be Greek or something?"

Cassie's criticism went unheeded, however, for the

youngest orphan was greatly admired at the actual ceremony, and Selina was congratulated by the Vicar's new wife.

"I am sure you will be a most successful dressmaker one day, Selina. All the ladies of the Colony will be clamoring for your advice."

Hearing this, Cassie escaped to the bottom of the vicarage garden, and in a most unladylike way climbed to the top of the old apple-tree. As far as she was concerned, the sooner they all set out for New South Wales, the better. Cassie had led a quiet and drab life when her parents were alive, a struggling existence brightened only by her morning visits to the vicarage school, where she had unexpectedly discovered that she was clever. Missabella was proud of Cassie's quickness to learn, and Cassie responded by working hard both in and out of school hours. Only now was she beginning to realize that all this aptitude might lead nowhere. If she were a boy, then it were just possible to win through to real scholarship, but what could a girl do? And here was Selina, who disliked books and loved sewing, being told that she had a promising future!

Cassie stayed in the apple-tree until the September sunlight was slanting low over the churchyard wall, and dreamt of a far new country where all doors were open to even the poorest and plainest of orphan girls.

First Steps on a Pilgrimage

IT WAS THE Vicar who first called them "Switherby's pilgrims," and, like pilgrims, they began their journey on foot. Missabella had planned carefully, working out times and connections so that as much money as possible might be saved with the minimum of discomfort to the children. She loved organizing anything, even the St. Matthew's Ladies' tea-parties, and the emigration scheme was a venture which she regarded as a true challenge to her capabilities. All Switherby was lost in awed admiration and respect for this small dowdy lady, no longer young, who proposed to set forth into the wilderness with ten dependent children and a very slim purse.

"I've told these lads to help you all they can, Ma'am," said Angus MacBain, as he handed over his two nephews. "Gavin is none too strong, but a change of air might make a braw lad out of him. Luke here can write a little, so if you'd ask him to drop me a letter now and then, I'd be grateful."

"Of course he shall write," said Missabella, giving ten-year-old Luke a stern glance. "And I intend to keep up their lessons whenever possible. Have they any luggage, Mr. MacBain?"

30

Their uncle displayed a bundle wrapped in a plaid.

"It's not much, but my poor brother Sandy had little enough to leave. He always rued the day he left Edinburgh, though there was no work for him there, either. He had a hankering after building things, Sandy did, and Gavin takes after him."

"Then I'll do my best to find work in that line for the boy," promised Missabella. "Perhaps you'll begin by building a house for all of us out there, Gavin."

Gavin half-smiled at what was apparently meant to be a friendly joke, but his face was gloomy again as he turned to take the bundle from his uncle. He understood only too well why Uncle Angus could no longer keep him and Luke in Switherby, for a bachelor miner living in cramped lodgings could hardly be expected to take care of two growing boys.

"But we're old enough to go and work at the mine with you," Gavin had pleaded. "We could save enough among all of us to go back to Edinburgh."

"Go back to what?" Angus had retorted. "To a hole in the wall down one of the wynds? You don't remember that, Gavin, and it's just as well. Besides, with that chest of yours you wouldn't last a year in the pits. I promised your father and mother I'd do my best for you, and as I see it, this offer of Miss Braithwaite's *is* the best."

So here they were, standing in the vicarage hallway on an October morning, while Uncle Angus made his awkward and reluctant farewells. As his large grimy figure finally receded, Gavin had to fight hard to prevent himself running after him.

"You may leave your caps and jackets in the schoolroom, boys —through this door. The other children are all out in the back garden, collecting the last of the fruit. I understand we need fresh fruit on a sea-voyage, although I'm afraid that among eleven of us it won't last very long."

The MacBains had been a habitually taciturn family, not given to idle chatter, so Missabella's loquacity was a surprise. In fact, almost everything about her was unexpected—her small stature, her unassuming mode of dress, her insignificance of feature allied with a remarkable self-confidence. The MacBain boys found themselves obeying her without question, and presently they were gathering up windfalls with the other orphans, albeit in a rather dazed fashion.

"You've come just in time, haven't you?" observed friendly Paul. "We leave at five o'clock this afternoon. And do you know that when we reach New South Wales it will be autumn again? Because they're all upside-down there."

"And there's no snow and hardly any fog," added Martha. "I can hardly believe *that.*"

"To think that this time tomorrow we shall be in Gravesend!" Cassie exclaimed. "Oh, I wish it were time to start!"

Somehow, Missabella, holding that too much excitement was bad for young constitutions, managed to make their departure as decorous as setting out for Morning Service on Sundays. The most agitated person present was the Vicar, despite the calm reassurances of his young wife.

"Arabella, are you certain you have all your papers safe?" he asked for the third time. "And please do write to us immediately if you are in any trouble."

"Of course, Hugh. But my letters will take so long to reach you that we will have plenty of time to sort out our troubles long before you hear of them. Now where is the man with the handcart?"

He was waiting by the backdoor, as ordered, and the hands of the tall old clock in the hall showed five minutes to five. Missabella had known the face and the chimes of that clock since childhood, and she had to give it one last affectionate pat.

"Don't forget to wind it, Hugh. And, Charlotte, I'm sure you will remember to water the begonias in the glasshouse—I was always rather proud of them. Come along, children."

The orphans, who had been ranged in a fidgetty line beside the staircase, gladly headed for the door. All were dressed in their warmest and heaviest garments, including a strange variety of headgear—the MacBains had plaid tam-o'-shanters, Selina a scarlet hood decorated with white braid, and Paul proudly sported a military-type high-crowned cap which his father had brought home from the wars. Switherby had been generous with its supply of knitted gloves and mufflers, but the chief problem had been the lack of shoes, and Robin had been obliged to don a pair of boots much too large for him. However, every orphan was shiningly clean and scrupulously neat, and even Cassie had brushed her hair so thoroughly that it hung in burnished strands over the collar of her dark cloak.

Such attention to appearance was duly rewarded, for quite a large number of the townsfolk had gathered in the market-square to give their pilgrims a fitting farewell. It was a miniature procession that they beheld, for Missabella came first in a new traveling outfit of olive-green broadcloth, her bulging reticule in one hand, and a prancing, blue-capped Sally-Lou firmly held by the other. The Vicar walked solemnly behind her, for he was to see the party on to the coach, and after him, in pairs, came eight more orphans. The ninth, Francis, by virtue of his seniority, marched along beside the handcart, which held all their luggage.

"God bless 'em!" cried an old lady. "And the very best of luck!"

Handkerchiefs were produced and used alternately for waving and for dabbing at eyes.

"Whatever are they crying about?" whispered Cassie to her partner, Marianne. "We're much luckier than they are— they have to stay in Switherby for ever and ever."

Selina was embarrassed by such a public display, and kept her gaze upon the cobbles at her feet. At the corner of the square, Missabella looked back once at the little brown church and the homely vicarage, both decked out now with the copper and gold of dying leaf, and then turned briskly down into the High Street.

"A little faster, children," she said. "We must on no account miss the coach."

It was about a mile across the fields to the Bingleton-London turnpike and the *Wheatsheaf Inn* where the pilgrims would board the coach. Missabella had chosen the night coach, as this would rule out the necessity of finding overnight accommodation in London, and would still allow them to arrive in Gravesend well before the specified time for embarkation.

"This is the farthest I've ever been from Switherby," announced Paul, as they climbed a stile between berry-hung hedges of hawthorn. "Once Mamma brought us here for a walk. Do you remember, Cassie?"

Cassie nodded, glancing back at the little town huddled along the hill-side. Factory smoke and autumn mist had combined to shroud its outlines so that it appeared unreal and distant, a smudged drawing without dimension. Ever afterwards she was to think of it thus, a dimmed October town with both its ugliness and its beauty melting into the golden landscape of the evening.

***

"What makes this place smell so queer?" asked Martha dubiously.

"It's the sea," answered Cassie. "Only, we can't really see it yet."

"Isn't that the sea, then?" demanded Paul. "It's big enough."

"It's part of the river—you know, the river we saw from London Bridge this morning. It's called the Thames."

Cassie was far too excited and interested to be tired. The younger children were heavy-eyed and dazed from lack of sleep, for the coach-journey had been long and jolting, and its sheer novelty had kept them awake. Breakfast had been a muddled meal of bread and cheese and apples, which Cook had packed the day before, and dinner a frugal repast in a cheap eating-house near the coaching station in London. The size and bustle of the city had subdued them all, even Missabella, and no one wished to linger there. But somehow Gravesend was not reassuring either, with its view of flat and foggy marsh, its bewildering array of masts and spars, and its decided coolness as the wind blew across the wharves straight off the river.

"I wish we could sit down somewhere," said Selina fretfully. "Only it's all so dirty."

"Missabella said to wait till she and Francis came back," Cassie said. "And to keep Sally-Lou away from the water."

Even Sally-Lou, however, had lost her zest. She huddled close to Cassie and sucked her thumb, her dark eyes sleepily following the flight of gulls over the dull green water. Robin had taken off his troublesome boots and was wriggling his toes idly on the planks of the wharf. Neither of the MacBains had spoken much during the journey, although Luke had become quite animated at the thought of highwaymen, and had looked for them at every halt. Now they were completely silent, with their tam-o'-shanters pulled down over their ragged black hair, and their short stocky bodies pressed against the scant shelter of a tumbledown shed.

Meanwhile, Missabella and Francis were doggedly searching for the *Medway Queen*. Neither of them had any but the sketchiest notion of shipping, and before them were all manner of craft from skiffs and barges to barques and frigates.

"We'll ask the next person we see," said Missabella determinedly, after fifteen minutes of fruitless peering at ships' hulls.

She was hoping to encounter someone with at least an air of authority, but all they could find just then was an ancient seaman perched on a bollard and smoking a very black and malodorous pipe.

"Excuse me," said Francis, seeing that Missabella would not approach too near, "but do you know a ship called the *Medway Queen?*

The seaman stared at Francis and spoke without removing the pipe.

"What sort of a ship'd she be?"

"I don't know exactly," Francis admitted. "But we're to sail to New South Wales in it—I mean her—so I suppose she must be quite big."

The seaman gave Francis a keen measuring glance in

which he obviously hinted that the boy was a landlubber indeed.

"Big? Dunno about that. If she's anywhere, she'll be over there."

He rose with a rheumaticky deliberation, and shuffled along the wharf. Missabella and Francis followed cautiously, for the planks were damp and slippery, and littered with sundry pieces of nautical gear. They passed several fishing-boats and a barge or two, then directly ahead Francis saw what surely must have been the largest and loveliest vessel that ever put to sea. She was a long graceful sweeping crea-ture, twin-decked, with three soaring masts that seemed to touch the flat grey sky. Her paint was spotless, her timbers whole and sound, her rigging a miracle of intricate effi-ciency.

Francis caught up with their guide.

"Is that her?" he asked eagerly. "Is that the *Medway Queen?*"

At last the seaman removed his pipe from his mouth, in order to utter a strange barking sound that was apparently a laugh.

"You ain't spent much time round ships, laddie. *That's* an East Indiaman, one of the fastest, too, and what's more she served with the Fleet in Lord Nelson's time. She's well over a thousand tons, without her guns."

"She's beautiful," said Francis, reverently, and this, at least, won the seaman's approval.

"That she is. This *Medway Queen*, now—would she be carrying lags?"

"I don't know," answered Francis, thinking this must be another unfamiliar nautical term.

"Lags—convicts—what else do they take to Botany Bay? Besides yerself, I mean."

"I suppose it could be a convict ship," admitted Francis. "But there are ten of us children, and Miss Braithwaite, so it must be a passenger ship too."

The seaman, evidently pondering the mystery of such a voluntary mass emigration, shook his head and peered into the distance.

"That might be her—can't make out the name, but she's the right sort o' shape."

Francis stared in the direction indicated.

"The little black boat over there? Are you sure?"

His escort spat thoughtfully over the edge of the wharf.

"Must be—she's the only other foreign-bound ship in the port. If yer want her proper name, she's a collier brig. A bit old, mebbe, but strong enough."

Missabella joined Francis, who pointed out the vessel that was to be their home for the next five months. She was squat and dirty, two-masted, and perhaps one hundred and twenty feet long. Her tonnage, so the seaman informed them, would be around three hundred and fifty.

For a few moments both Francis and Missabella gazed at the *Medway Queen* in silent dismay. It had begun to rain, a fine foggy drizzle that fused river and sky into one colorless and cheerless whole. Missabella gave one shiver, and pulled herself together.

"Go back and fetch the others, Francis, and take this fellow here to help with the baggage." She jiggled her reticule so that a few coins clinked. "I'll go aboard and see the captain. Hurry, now— we must get into shelter."

But what kind of shelter would it be? Twenty minutes later the ten orphans were trying to find the answer, as they filed on board under the unenthusiastic scrutiny of Will Trimble, Master of the *Medway Queen*. After a dozen years

on the Botany Bay run, Captain Trimble had become accustomed to a variety of cargoes, animal, vegetable, and
mineral, and nowadays he was not easily startled or disturbed. He accepted all his passengers, including the convicts, with a calm indifference, reserving his anxieties—and
his choicest language—for the vagaries of the weather and
the behavior of his rascally crew. Indeed, he had long since
decided that convicts were far less trouble than free emigrants, the former being in no position to make tedious
demands upon an overworked and underpaid captain. He
was an unsociable old bachelor who loved his ship, creaky
cantankerous tub that she was, and was far more skilled in
her management than in the handling of people.

" 'Ow many little 'uns is there?" demanded the mate,
scowling at the procession of orphans.

" 'Bout ten," grunted the captain. "And everyone will be
sea-sick, I'll be bound."

"Pity they 'adn't all stayed 'ome," observed the mate.

Missabella was strongly inclined to share his opinion, had
he but known it. When the captain showed her the quarters to be shared by her and the children, she was for once
in her life at a loss for words, and by the time she had recovered her powers of speech, the captain was back on deck.

"I'm sure there must be some mistake," she declared. "This
can't be meant for *all* of us."

The orphans crowded behind her into a cabin some ten
feet square, with the decking overhead sloping to a height
of about five and a half feet on the seaward side. One narrow scuttle let in a faint light and a strong odor of salt and
decaying fish. There were two double bunks, and an array
of hooks for slinging hammocks, and that was all.

But the old seaman, their temporary baggage-porter,

looked about in approval.

"Pretty neat, ain't it? Yer should 'ave seen our crew's quarters when I was a lad."

"We are not crew," Missabella pointed out coldly.

" 'Course not, Ma'am. They sling their hammocks in the fo'c'sle. This 'ere's amidships."

"Francis, help this fellow put our baggage in the corner. I shall go and see the captain."

After ten minutes of argument on Missabella's part, and of passive resistance from Captain Trimble, it was the listening mate who provided some sort of solution.

"Them three big boys can sleep in the old gun-bay next to the cabin. Plenty o' room for three 'ammocks there."

"That still leaves eight of us in that tiny cabin," protested Missabella.

This was altogether too much for the captain.

"Tiny, you say? Ma'am, that's the best accommodation we've got anywhere on the ship, and you're lucky to have it. You won't find any better on the New South Wales run."

Missabella could recognize defeat when it really stared her in the face. She had to accept the mate's offer, and return to her charges.

They were all rapidly recovering their spirits now that they were actually on board.

"When do we sail?" clamored the younger children. "Is it tonight?"

"No, not tonight, but probably tomorrow," said Missabella. "Tonight we shall all go early to bed and get used to our bunks and our hammocks before we are really at sea."

As it turned out, they had not one, but three nights in which to sample their strange beds while still in port.

Captain Trimble was vague and evasive when pressed to give the sailing date.

"My letter from the Colonial Secretary says the fifth of October," Missabella said grandly, on the first morning. "That was yesterday."

"I know that, Ma'am, but we can't sail till we're loaded up and provisioned," explained the captain with what scant patience he could summon. "Our cargoes haven't arrived yet, and the ship's chandler didn't turn up on time, neither."

The next day Missabella tackled the mate, who was more affable but no more definite.

"Could be the day after termorrer. The convicts should be 'ere in the mornin', then we'll load the cargoes."

But at least the mate proved helpful in one respect. He checked Missabella's own stores, and found them sadly deficient for a voyage of four to five months.

"I'll take a couple o' them lads ashore an' get the storekeeper to send up some more stuff. Can yer trust the biggest boy with the money?"

"Of course," said Missabella, turning to Francis. "Buy just what the mate tells you, and make sure you're not cheated by the shopkeeper."

"No chance o' that with me around," growled the mate, and Francis well believed him, for Josh Greentree was a burly, bearded fellow from Rotherhithe, who had been at sea for twenty of his thirty years.

Fortunately the weather improved sufficiently for the orphans to spend most of their waiting-time on deck, where they skipped from one chosen spot to another to avoid the crew, who were in a collective bad temper as the sailing date grew closer, and were likely to swear heartily at any child who happened to be in the way.

"On no account are any of you to go near the fo'c'sle," warned Missabella sternly. "The less you see of these ruffians, the better."

But Missabella's vigilance did not prevent some of the orphans from witnessing a sight truly remarkable and distressing to creatures from a remote country town. On the afternoon of their second day in the port, Cassie, Paul, and Robin were leaning over the gunwale amidships, watching the loading of assorted tools and black-smithing equipment destined for the tradesmen of Sydney Town. Missabella had taken the others for a short walk on the wharf, but Robin's boots were still troubling him, and Cassie and Paul had elected to watch him in Missabella's absence.

"Aren't there going to be any other passengers?" asked Paul. "I haven't seen any yet."

"There won't be much room left, I'm sure," said Cassie, who was marveling at the amount of cargo being taken on. "Where would they sleep? Every little corner is full up."

"I can see people coming now," declared Paul, leaning outwards at an angle which would have appalled Missabella. "They look like soldiers."

On the clutter of the wharf the bright red of soldiers' coats was startling enough, but it soon became evident that the soldiers were but escorts to an extraordinary procession, a long shuffling, ragged file of grey-clad men, dirty and unshaven, chained together in pairs. Along the wharf and on the ships seamen fell silent, and watched sombrely as the soldiers directed the clanking band towards the *Medway Queen*.

"It's the convicts!" cried Cassie. "Get back, Paul!"

"Why? They can't hurt me," Paul objected. "Anyway, they're going in that other way, down below."

"That's where they load the stores and cargo," said Cassie. "How can they put people in there too?"

Despite a chilly sort of distaste, that was almost fear, Cassie felt compelled to look down at the unattractive figures now being half-pushed into the hold. These were people, after all, and not animals, and how could they possibly spend the entire voyage in that black and evil-smelling cavern below the water-line? And how would she ever sleep at night, knowing they were there? Her rather hard and narrow bunk suddenly seemed like the most luxurious couch.

She became aware that Robin was tugging at her arm and trying to say something. He, too, had seen the convicts, and Cassie noticed with astonishment that his peaked little face, always strangely old for a child's countenance, had gone completely white.

"What is it, Robin? What's the matter?"

But all Robin would say, again and again, was the one word: "Father," at the same time pointing towards the wharf. He was in such a state of terror that Cassie hardly knew what to do.

"What does he mean?" asked Paul. "Is his father one of the soldiers?"

"I don't think so," said Cassie, examining the upright and tidy men in scarlet and white. She had never seen Josiah Gracechurch; however, she had often overheard scraps of whispered gossip about him in the Switherby streets, talk which suggested that his inevitable destination was the county jail. Nothing had been heard of him for months now, and the twins never mentioned him. Robin could so easily have been mistaken, and seen just a passing resemblance to his father in one of those grey figures.

"You didn't really see your father, Robin," she told him, clutching his cold hands. "He couldn't be here. Look, Missabella's coming with the others—she won't let anyone hurt you."

Missabella had seen the approach of the convicts from afar, and hurried back to make sure that none of her charges had been disturbed by such a sight. One glance at Cassie and Robin informed her that she was too late. Cassie explained the reason for Robin's agitation while his sisters took him below.

"How very odd!" remarked Missabella, frowning. "I'm certain Robin must have been imagining the whole thing, but we must be careful lest he should see the convicts again during the voyage. I understand they are brought up on deck from time to time for exercise."

Cassie looked down at the soldiers now standing guard at the entrance to the hold.

"Missabella, what did all those men do to be sent to Botany Bay?"

"I don't believe we should go into that now," said Missabella firmly. "I'll try to tell you all about it one day when you're older. Isn't it time for you to take the kettle along to the galley for our tea?"

By noon the next day the incident was forgotten, for at last Captain Trimble gave the order to set sail. The wind was in the right quarter, the tide was on the turn. With protesting creaks and groans, the old *Medway Queen* swung out into midstream, and pointed her bows towards the other side of the world.

 4

Interlude at Sea

THERE IS PERHAPS only one benefit conferred upon the traveler who spends between four and five months at sea in a small and overcrowded vessel. With the passing of each day, his destination becomes more and more desirable, until in his mind it is nothing short of the earthly paradise, and he will in all probability never leave it for the rest of his life.

Thus it was with the ten Switherby orphans and their guardian. They endured autumn gales in the Bay of Biscay, were becalmed beneath an equatorial sun on the way from Tenerife to Rio de Janeiro, and had their drinking-water rationed in the Indian Ocean. The captain's dire prophecy was fulfilled before the ship reached the North Foreland, and all the children were sea-sick. So, unfortunately, was Missabella, and for one week she sincerely regretted her decision to depart from the glorious stability of the vicarage. In that first week, with the entire party laid low, Josh Greentree was their unlikely savior, stumping into the cabin whenever his duties permitted, and distributing hot tea, dry biscuit, and seaman-like advice to his wretched passengers.

On the eighth day, Marianne and Martha struggled to

their feet and came to the mate's assistance. The Bay of Biscay was behind them, and the ship's movement had subsided to a steady roll, instead of the hectic tossing and pitching in which she had so recently indulged.

"All them as is better, up on deck," ordered Josh next morning, and soon a wavering quartet, consisting of the twins, Francis and Selina, was making its way into the strangeness of sunlight above. In the afternoon they were joined by Gavin, Luke, and Paul, and next day by Robin and Sally-Lou, who regained her spirits so rapidly that she had to have a nursemaid appointed in turn from the ranks of the older children, to prevent her from falling overboard. For by now the children were discovering that the sea had its delights after all; as the *Medway Queen* sailed southward, the waves flattened out into long glassy, turquoise rollers, and the sun beat down with a warmth more potent than the Switherby pilgrims could have believed possible.

Missabella recovered more slowly, and Cassie was the last, by several days, to find her sea-legs. This annoyed her considerably; it was galling to know that Selina, for all her seeming delicacy and airs and graces, made a better sailor than Cassie. As the weeks passed Selina bloomed into real beauty, her skin dyed a pale soft brown, her flying hair shining like silver in the tropical light. She forgot for the time being to be refined and ladylike; she joined in the games with the smaller children and took a real interest in the lessons which Missabella gave on deck every morning. Francis and Selina became firm friends, and Cassie, always given to brooding in silence over her grievances, fell into a prolonged bout of sulks.

Of the others, Martha and Marianne were the cabin housekeepers, forever tidying and cleaning, sorting clothes—

the winter outfits were now entirely discarded—and keeping a vigilant eye on the stores' chest, lest any greedy orphan might be tempted to help himself between meals. Physical drudgery was nothing new to the Gracechurch girls, for they had known little else at home, but now they were working to please their friends, and their delight in Missabella's words of praise brought color to their cheeks and brightness to their eyes.

"I can see you are both going to be worth your weight in gold, once we've settled in New South Wales," said Missabella. "Why, even the captain remarked on the neat appearance of our cabin!"

This was indeed an unwonted tribute from Captain Trimble, who avoided his passengers most of the time. The children alarmed him with their noise and their liveliness, all except Gavin MacBain. Like the captain, Gavin was a fellow of few words and rare smiles, but he had a way with tools, and the captain, having not enough crew to go round, soon allowed Gavin to attend to various little repair jobs about the ship. Clad in ragged trousers and a seaman's ancient jacket, his over-long black hair stiff with salt, Gavin pottered around contentedly, even whistling sea-shanties when he thought no one would hear him. His younger brother Luke, a little more talkative and not quite so much inclined for hard work, preferred to spend his leisure hours following Josh about the ship, and acquiring, as well as a knowledge of the technicalities of sails and rigging, a species of vocabulary unknown even in the wynds of Edinburgh.

As usual, Robin stayed close to the other children and watched and listened, content with the occasional comment or smile directed towards him. For the first week of the voyage, he had been prone to nightmares in which he apparently dreamt of his father, but soon the novelty of ship-board life and the constant presence of his sisters and friends brought him reassurance. Thanks to Missabella's alertness, none of the children ever saw the convicts at their exercise, and it was only Cassie who continued to speculate on that wretched human cargo down below.

But no matter how the children strove in their various ways to occupy themselves, their enthusiasms had waned considerably by the middle of February. They had then been at sea for four and a half months—they had put in at several ports, certainly, but Missabella, carefully hoarding her money and in any case highly suspicious of foreign hygiene and food, had not taken any of the children ashore. The long haul across the Indian Ocean was apparently without end; it was late summer in this part of the world, they were told, yet how could seasons mean anything at all when there was no visible land? All that varied was the color of the sea, or the shape of the clouds in the sky. One night Josh took the older orphans on deck to show them the Southern Cross; it was simply a collection of stars, however, and not at all the flaming vivid cross that Cassie, at least, had expected.

"Watch out for flyin' fish any day now," Josh advised not long afterwards, and all the children spent an afternoon competing for the largest number spotted, but soon their eyes ached with the effort of following those darting shapes from wave to wave, and they abandoned the pastime, all except Paul, who took the keenest interest in every form of bird and sea life. He even tried to tame a gull that trailed the *Medway Queen* for days—he was positive that it was always the same gull, though the others scoffed at him.

Only Captain Trimble seemed to have any clear idea of southern geography. Josh Greentree, when asked one morning whether the dim grey blur on the horizon to port was part of New Holland, merely scratched his head and looked doubtful.

"Dunno, Miss. It's a pretty big country, like. An' even if it is New 'olland, there's still lots of sea between us an' Port Jackson."

Wearily, the orphans settled back into the old routine of lessons and walks round the deck, sleep, and meals. These last had become the dreariest features of the day, for there was nothing left to eat but shriveled biscuits and a few scraps of salt beef. Water was rationed, and only two brews of tea per day were allowed—even the youngest child, Sally-Lou, learned to savor the strong black liquid right to the dregs.

It was evening on the last day of February, in a dark ominous rising sea, that Cassie, always scanning the horizon, noticed something to starboard that was neither cloud nor water, but more solid than both.

"It *must* be land," she declared to Francis. "But how did it get over there?"

"We'll ask Josh," said Francis, glancing up towards the quarterdeck, where the mate was directing operations on the stern mast. This was forbidden territory to all the children except Francis and Gavin, who were sometimes summoned there to run messages for the captain. By the time Francis had struggled up and down the companion-way, the horizon was completely hidden by a curtain of rain, and aft of the wildly tossing ship the sun was sinking into stormy dull crimson cloud.

"Josh said, get below this minute," Francis shouted over the crashing of waves and the violent creaking of timbers. "It's Van Diemen's Land, he thinks, but we can't put in because of the weather, so we're going to run for Port

Jackson."

It was hardly a run, however—more of a laborious crawl. The waters of Bass Strait were high and wild in a series of late-summer storms, which filled the *Medway Queens* water-casks, certainly, but gave Captain Trimble many anxious moments as he fought to keep his old craft on course, and to avoid running aground on the reefs of this treacherous coast. When at last they left the Strait and headed northward, they were met by an unfriendly headwind which further delayed their progress.

On a bulkhead in the cabin, Missabella had hung a calendar, on which she canceled out each of the passing days. It was ragged now, and splotched with salt-water where the waves had caught it on those occasions when the scuttle had not been closed in time. Early one morning, Missabella was crossing off the third of March, before making the few preparations for a meager breakfast. She was not quite the spruce and brisk Miss Braithwaite who had left St. Matthew's vicarage five months previously; her grey dress was stained and bedraggled, and for the first time in her life she was feeling twinges of rheumatism—a disgrace, she considered, for a woman in the prime of life.

She turned to bid Selina fetch the other children for breakfast —as usual at this hour, they were all on deck, but Selina was on cabin duty, which meant stowing hammocks and tidying the bunks. She drooped a little as she worked, for she hated the cabin now, with its stuffy stale odor, its plague of black-beetles, and its depressing lack of light. Selina spent a great deal of time lately dreaming of the ancestral castle in Northumberland, and of the fine relatives who surely would one day trace her and take her joyfully home to those gleaming halls of marble.

"Missabella, come quick! You can see it—you can see Port Jackson!"

Several orphans tumbled into the cabin, and Cassie danced wildly in the middle of the floor while Paul shouted the news. What a sight was Cassie, thought Selina distastefully, and how clumsy she looked, with her shabby holland frock inches above her ankles, and her hair in long wisps about her face. Why, the people of Sydney Town would surely take her for a female convict!

But only Selina could pay any regard to personal appearances just then. Even Missabella so far forgot herself as to rush on deck still wearing her apron. Ignored, Selina set about getting the breakfast.

Overnight, the whole atmosphere aboard the *Medway Queen*— except perhaps in the hold—had altered from one of gloomy resignation to relief and hope. Captain Trimble was actually smiling as he brought his ship about to enter the port. Even the wind had changed, and was now blowing gently but helpfully from the east.

"Isn't it the loveliest morning!" cried Cassie, leaning over the port rail. "Look, Paul—did you ever see such cliffs? And there's a lighthouse—do you see it?"

Paul nodded, trying to gaze in all directions at once. Any land at all would have been a truly glorious sight to the weary orphans, but what they beheld now was a promising vision indeed. To port and starboard towered great grey foam-skirted headlands, the portside one bearing the lighthouse, the other crested with dark-green heath. So brilliant and clear was the light on this cloudless March morning, that the landscape seemed quite subdued in color, but as the harbor opened out, inside the heads, the patterns of the foreshores appeared delicately etched in pale-gold sand, and here and there were bright patches of paint-box hues where gardens bloomed on the slopes, amid the universal grey-green of native bush.

"Shall we live in a house like that?" asked Paul hopefully, indicating a long graceful stone building on a near-by point. As far as he was concerned, a whole age had passed since their departure from Switherby, and now anything seemed possible, even for a small orphan without a penny in his pockets.

"Indeed we shall not," said Missabella firmly, for it was certainly not her policy to encourage notions of grandeur. "We shall be lucky to have any roof at all over our heads. That house probably belongs to an English gentleman of means, and means, Paul, are what we do *not* have."

"All the same," Cassie said to her younger brother when their guardian had gone below again, "I don't see why we shouldn't be rich one day. I've read stories about very humble people making their fortunes in the colonies—even convicts. So why shouldn't we?"

Cassie longed to stay on deck until their arrival at Sydney Cove, but she could not escape Missabella so easily. No matter how rapidly Cassie gulped her breakfast, almost scalding her mouth with her tea, it was of no avail. There were preparations to be made for disembarkation, and all the orphans must assist. First their few belongings had to be stowed in the old Army bags they had brought from Switherby, and collected in a heap together with the trunks which had remained locked during the voyage— these held all the blankets and bedding, the tools and hardware, and sundry other items donated by the good folk of Switherby.

"We shall have to ask Josh to help with those," said Missabella. "And now I want all you children to dress in your traveling clothes, and make yourselves as clean and neat as possible. Whatever happens, we must remember to behave like proper young ladies and gentlemen."

Grumbling under her breath, Cassie dragged out the clothes she had worn for the coach journey to Gravesend. The blue woollen frock and matching cloak were the only good garments she possessed, and even she could recognize the unsuitability of arriving in Sydney Town in her out-grown and faded holland, but nonetheless it was a sore trial to be decked out in wool and barathea on such a sunny morning. As she braided her thick unruly hair, she stood as close as she dared to the scuttle, and by twisting this way and that, she managed to catch tantalizing glimpses of scenery slowly gliding past—a green hill with a windmill, a rocky point, an odd-looking conical island. What a large harbor this must be! It was well past breakfast-time, and still they had not reached the wharf.

"Cassie, please tie Robin's bootlaces, and brush his hair," said Missabella. "When you are all ready, you will go in pairs on to the deck, and wait for me. The older ones will carry the Army bags."

Selina hoped fervently that not many people would be about to witness their arrival, for she hated to be part of the strange little procession. Her partner *would* have to be Cassie, who had grown considerably during the voyage, and was at least half a head taller than Selina, and as fidgetty as a young colt. But fortunately Francis led the group, and he was sedate and tidy and handsome enough to satisfy Selina's standards.

They arrived on deck just as the *Medway Queen* was edging into the wharf. There were indeed many townsfolk gathered on the shores of the little semi-circular bay, for the coming of any vessel from England was still an event of some significance in the settlement. Soldiers were ranged on the wharf itself, no doubt to receive the travelers from the hold, and a few ragged children—scantily and comfortably dressed, as Cassie noted with envy—were perched on bollards and coils of rope, from which they were soon unceremoniously evicted.

No one had come to welcome the orphans, of course—the Appletons lived somewhere near a place queerly named Parramatta, and in any case their interest in Miss Braithwaite's collection of waifs was tenuous indeed. None of the children except Selina was at all dismayed by this, for the sight of acre upon acre of real solid immovable land was delight enough.

"I could run and jump and skip for *hours*," said Cassie restlessly. "There's plenty of room—this place is not a bit crowded and cramped like Switherby."

Immediately before them there were a number of buildings, some of considerable size and grandeur, some small and modest, and to right and left the slopes had been transformed into a semblance of urban order, but as one looked farther, and over one's shoulder at the land on the northern side of the harbor, it was not difficult to remember that the settlement was not yet forty years old. Not even the warmth of the sun and the calm benevolence of the sky could quite dispel the feeling that Sydney Town was merely a small speck on the edge of a vast and old and unpredictable continent.

The orphans were accustomed to waiting more or less resignedly for whatever might come next, but this morning the delay was undoubtedly galling. The ship was tied up, the gangplank was down—*why* did Missabella not come? When she finally appeared, she was talking to Josh

Greentree, and neither of them seemed to be in a hurry at all.

The matter under discussion was an important one, however—where were they all to live while they were in Sydney? Nobody could say for certain just how long it would take for the land grant to be finalized.

"I dunno as 'ow I could reckermend the part of town us seamen know," Josh was saying. "We favor Bunker's 'ill, Ma'am, over there—"

He waved his cap towards the headland on the west side of the cove, indicating an area between the Army barracks and the gun-battery on the point.

"Not a place to take all them little 'uns to," he observed, though not, rather to Cassie's disappointment, giving any reasons. "Come to think of it, though, I 'ave a friend workin' at a very respectable sort o' place in Chapel Row—a boardin'- 'ouse, like. I can't get ashore meself, but I'll tell yer 'ow to get there."

From her reticule Missabella took an address-book which was to become very familiar to the orphans in the next few weeks. Josh could neither write nor spell, but between the two of them the name and whereabouts of the boarding- house were committed to paper. Missabella then transferred a coin or two from her bag to the mate's hand, and Josh touched his battered cap in respectful farewell. The children clustered around with their own less restrained good- byes, and Sally-Lou shocked both Missabella and Selina by hugging the ship's mate with the greatest affection.

"All the same," admitted Missabella, as they turned at last towards the gangplank, "I believe our voyage would have been far less comfortable without his help. Now, Francis, we must ask one of these lads to find us a handcart, and take our trunks to Chapel Row. It's over this way."

She gestured confidently towards a section of the town where a graceful spire rose among deep-green trees, and dutifully and hopefully the children set out in that direction.

Josh Greentree and several idle bystanders were not, after all, the only ones to see the Switherby party go forth on the next stage of their pilgrimage. The convicts were being led out of the hold, and one of them, whose eyes had had time to grow accustomed to the brilliant light, was standing on the wharf in his chains, staring after Missabella and her crocodile. Josiah Gracechurch had not beheld his children for almost a year, but there was no mistaking the twins, nor little Robin with his limp—although the boy was plumper and more cheerful than his father remembered.

"Well, I'll be—" said Josiah to himself. "How's that for luck?"

Convicted criminal he might be, sentenced to transportation for ten years for theft, yet his cunning had not left him during the hideous voyage, nor his optimism. Already a plan was beginning to take shape in his mind, and he continued to gaze after the children meditatively until the last small pair of figures was completely gone from sight.

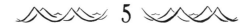# 5

Plans and Purchases

"WHOEVER'S UP THAT tree, come down this minute! Missabella wants all of us, *now!*"

The branches of the tall pine shook above Selina's shining head, and a pair of thin and bony ankles slid into view, followed by the hem of a ragged skirt.

"Really, Cassie, don't you know there are people watching?" Selina asked in her primmest voice. "Anyone would think you were in the middle of the country."

"I wish I was," said Cassie, unrepentant. "We've been here two weeks already, and it's nothing but manners, manners, all the time. What does Missabella want us for?"

"I don't know. She's on the back porch, and there are three of us missing. Two now—Paul and Robin."

"I'll soon find them," promised Cassie. She gave a perfunctory pat to her hair, and set off along the street at a sort of restrained trot. It was hard to realize that Chapel Row was actually part of a town, with its unpaved surface deeply rutted by cart and coach wheels, and its houses and shops built in so many different styles and materials. There were some fine new stone buildings, to be sure, such as the Supreme Court, and several neat brick cottages and a couple

57

of tidy little inns, but the presence of a blacksmith's shop, and a number of dwellings in timber of uncertain origin, somehow suggested a remote country village. Indeed, Mrs. Peachey's boarding-house itself had a rustic air, with its uneven shingled roof, its sprawling garden, and its grape-vine trained over the front porch. Three pine-trees stood in front of it, and it was in one of these that Cassie had been perched, enjoying an excellent view of Sydney from the Racecourse in the east to the barracks in the west.

About a hundred yards away, on the opposite side of the street, was a well where most of the local inhabitants drew their drinking-water. It was a favorite spot for gatherings and for gossip, and Cassie had noticed Susannah leaving Mrs. Peachey's premises earlier with two small boys, all three carrying buckets. Susannah was the boarding-house maid-servant, and Josh Greentree's friend —all the children en-joyed her company and her extravagant tales of her adven-turous life. None of the orphans had yet seen fit to reveal to Missabella that Susannah had arrived in the Colony as a convict; to them, it was merely an added dash of romance to embellish her stories, but they all dimly understood that Missabella's standards were still those of St. Matthew's vic-arage.

Paul and Robin had filled their buckets with as much water as they could carry, and were sitting on the stone cop-ing of the well, listening to a conversation between Susannah and the barmaid from the *Cherry Tree* inn. That the talk was of a highly diverting nature was evident from Paul's wide and wondering eyes, and from Robin's concentrated attention. Cassie would have liked to linger and listen her-self, but an annoying sense of responsibility, growing more insistent of late, prevented her.

"Missabella wants you," she told the boys. "And you'd better put your shoes on, Paul."

Only Robin was permitted to go barefoot, as long as the weather was mild, for his old boots had been discarded, and funds did not stretch to a new pair. So he jogged along happily in the dust, now and then waving a hand shyly in return to a greeting from a window or a porch-step—almost everyone in Chapel Row knew Robin, just as everyone was familiar with the history of the orphans in general. Susannah was no doubt partly responsible for this state of affairs, which pleased most of the children and rather alarmed Missabella.

"What does she want us for?" asked Paul. "We aren't starting lessons again yet, are we?"

"I don't know," answered Cassie. "But she's been to the Secretary's office this morning, so it could be about the land grant."

"I'd like to stay here," said Paul, who had had enough of moves and journeys. "Mrs. Peachey makes the best muffins in the world, and we can have cream on our porridge every day."

"It costs too much—I heard Missabella say so. Besides, don't you want to get out into the country and do some exploring? That's what we came for."

"Susannah says people come to New South Wales because they're not wanted at home. Isn't *that* why we came?"

But fortunately for Cassie, who found this question rather awkward, they had reached Mrs. Peachey's gate, and she hustled the boys inside without more ado. The wide central hallway was dim and cool, and smelt deliciously of beefsteak pudding; after the privations of the voyage, all the children were taking a keen interest in food, and Paul gave a quick glance at the clock to see how long it was till dinner-time.

The back porch was an unpretentious affair, with uneven floorboards, and wooden posts supporting both a sagging roof and a vigorous Bougainvillaea vine. The five boys all slept here—at a slightly reduced rate—and now Missabella sat bold upright on the edge of one of the beds, with her charges seated in a semicircle on the floor. Francis, Gavin and Selina were all looking expectant, so Cassie guessed that some important news was indeed forthcoming. She hoped that Missabella would not be too long in the telling of it—more than any of them Cassie longed to be up and away, meeting the adventures that she felt certain lay ahead.

"I shan't keep you younger children very long," Missabella began. "I shall need the older ones, however, because you should understand exactly what we are going to do. You have all heard me speak of a grant of land—it is given to free settlers in the Colony under certain conditions. I could not specify any particular district, of course, and I'm afraid we shall be traveling a little farther than I had expected."

Paul groaned at this, but Cassie gazed at Missabella with intense interest.

"How will we get there?" demanded Luke, with vivid memories of the *Medway Queen*.

"I shall come to that in a moment. The land consists of sixty acres—a modest size for this country, but quite sufficient for us— about ninety miles south of here, near the coast."

"Do you mean, the Governor gives us all that land for nothing?" asked Francis, immediately seeing Governor Darling as the most generous and benevolent of men, an opinion contrary to that held by the Colony as a whole.

"Not exactly for nothing. Within five years we must have so much of it cultivated, or else forfeit it. That means, Paul, we must work on it or give it up."

The older orphans were silent, trying to grasp the implications of Missabella's statement. None of them had any idea of the extent of one acre, let alone sixty, but they could vaguely understand that a great deal of hard work lay before them. To Cassie and Francis, it was exciting, to Selina bewildering, and to Gavin, whose skills were mostly in his hands, most gratifying.

"We shall have one convict assigned to us as a laborer," went on Missabella. "I can only hope that he turns out to be reliable, for there will be some work that could prove too much for us on our own."

Plainly, Gavin and Cassie did not believe her—both felt equal to moving mountains, if necessary.

"We shall be leaving just as soon as we have made a few essential purchases, and probably we shall travel by dray, as I understand the road is very rough. And now, Martha, you and Marianne may take the smaller children for a short walk before dinner—no speaking to strangers, mind."

Luke decided for the moment to classify himself as a junior member of the group, and slipped away before Gavin could summon him back. Gavin had been told by his uncle always to look after Luke, and Gavin took his responsibilities seriously, as he did everything. Luke was a high-spirited boy, however, and lately had begun to follow his own inclinations, which were mostly towards athletic pursuits—he was growing tall and strong for his age, and enjoyed matching his muscles with those of the other boys in the street.

Missabella contemplated the solemn faces of the four

remaining children. It was difficult to think of them any longer as children, although the oldest, Francis, was only just thirteen. On Francis in particular Missabella had come to depend; therefore the decision she had recently made had been rendered doubly hard.

"It may not be possible for all of us to leave Sydney together," she said, with a hesitation unusual indeed in one so forthright. "Your education has to be considered, Francis."

"Why can't I do lessons with the others?" asked Francis in surprise.

His sister, always the quicker of the two, guessed what Missabella had in mind, and with all her heart rebelled against this first breaking-up of the orphan family. Knowing that Missabella would have the final say, Cassie edged closer to her brother.

"I'm afraid, Francis, that I am no longer capable of teaching you all you need to learn. Your parents wanted more than anything else a good education for you, and a fair start in life. These you won't have on a farm thirty miles from the nearest school."

"It doesn't matter—" Francis began despairingly, but Missabella hurried on.

"I have gone into the matter very carefully, and if you can obtain a place at the Free Grammar School, Mrs. Peachey will kindly allow you to live here at special rates. She is a good woman, and I can trust her to look after you."

Francis cast one glance of appeal at Cassie, for he himself could never express his deep horror of Missabella's proposal. How *could* he stay here alone, for years perhaps, while the others went out to shape a farm in the wilderness? For *that* was the substance of Francis' dream—not a life of scholarship and financial security, but the management of a farm, the ownership of a few acres where he could watch his crops grow, and tend his animals. To Francis Brown of Switherby, such an ambition would have been hopeless, and too ludicrous to be mentioned; here, however, it had come almost within his grasp, only to be snatched away because his mother had confided very different plans to the vicar's sister.

"He *can't* stay here by himself," pleaded Cassie. "He doesn't know anybody but us. I'll help him with his lessons, if you'll only let him come."

She so far forgot her rigid pride as to clutch at Missabella's hands. Even Selina was moved to add her plea to Cassie's, and Gavin regarded Francis with mute but very real sympathy. Missabella had to resort to her severest voice and expression, hitherto reserved for the perpetrators of major acts of mischief and disobedience.

"That will do, girls. My mind is made up, and I cannot forget my duty towards your father and mother, Francis. I am sure you will study hard, and in a few years will be in a position to support yourself, and even return to England if you so wish."

Francis hardly wished that at the moment. But being a reserved and docile boy, he swallowed his misery, and refused to allow Cassie to make any further mention of the subject to Missabella.

"It won't do any good," he said. "She thinks she's doing her best for me, you see. She doesn't understand that I'm old enough to make up my own mind."

"It will be awful without you," declared Cassie, whose thoughts were now veering to her personal prospects, instead of her brother's. "Gavin hardly ever talks, and Luke hasn't any sense, and Selina is impossible."

"She's all right, if you'd only try and make friends with her. Don't you realize that once you're on the farm, you'll see nobody but yourselves? You'll just have to get on with one another."

This was indeed an entirely new idea to Cassie, and with its suggestion of the orphans' becoming rather like castaways on a desert island, it quite appealed to her imagination. Somehow, the coming parting with Francis was almost forgotten in the next few days, for once again the Switherby pilgrims were plunged into a frenzy of preparation. Missabella spent hours poring over her account books and the pages of the *Sydney Gazette*, which advertised for sale such indispensable items as muskets—"Gavin must learn how to shoot"—hatchets, saws, fishing-rods, seed potatoes, tarpaulins, and all kinds of livestock. This last really posed a problem for Missabella, whose knowledge of animals was limited to the care of domestic cats.

"I expect we *should* have a cat, to keep down the mice," she observed. "I'm sure we'll easily find a stray kitten, but however am I to buy a cow? And I've no notion what horses cost."

It was Paul who indirectly provided the solution. He had gone with Susannah to the well early one misty morning, the first morning with a definite autumn chill in the air, and lingered while she gossiped with the blacksmith's daughter. Presently he heard the ringing note of horses' hooves on the pebbles, and moved away to the stone trough to see the animal being watered. A well-dressed middle-aged gentleman dismounted, and tossed the reins to the boy.

"Hold him for a minute, lad. I shan't be long."

He strode into one of the buildings opposite, leaving Paul to admire the sleek flanks of his steed, and to wonder whether Missabella would be likely to purchase such an attractive animal. A few weeks of colonial life had given Paul a new confidence, so when the man returned, he spoke up boldly:

"Please sir, how much does it cost to buy a horse like this one?"

The stranger stopped searching in his pockets for a suitable coin (which in any case Paul would have had to refuse, so sound was Missabella's training) and studied his young questioner in amusement.

"Are you thinking of buying him? He's not for sale."

"Oh, no, sir," answered Paul seriously. "I can see you think a great deal of him. But we need a horse, because we're going to live on a farm. Well, a sort of farm, only we have to make it one ourselves."

The gentleman stroked his chin, and invited Paul to give him the whole story. Seeing that Susannah was still occupied, Paul obliged.

"That's most interesting," said the man, without sarcasm. "You seem to have some spirit, all of you, and I should like to help. Here—give this card to your guardian, and ask her if I may call around eleven. You're at Mrs. Peachey's, you say? No, you needn't show me—I know her place. Her late husband bought that land from me, as a matter of fact."

The engraved printing on the card was beyond Paul's powers of deciphering, but there was no doubt that it favorably impressed both Missabella and Mrs. Peachey.

"Mr. Thomas Rose?" echoed the latter, pausing in the middle of the porridge-ladling—to Paul's frustration, for he was very hungry after his outing. "Why, he used to own most of the land hereabouts. Did very well for himself, and settled on a big place out at Appin. Calls it Mount Gilead."

Missabella produced a map that she had had copied from one in the Surveyor-General's office.

"How fortunate—Appin is not so far at all from our own destination. In fact," added Missabella, peering more closely at the map, "it appears to be the only settlement of any size anywhere near us. Dear me, I cannot get used to the colonial idea of distance —in this country, forty miles is but a short step."

"What's the name of this place you're going to, then?" asked Mrs. Peachey, who had not been farther than Parramatta during her fifteen years of residence in the Colony, and even then had gone in mortal terror of the unseen black men.

"It has no name yet, but the whole district seems to be called the Illawarra," explained Missabella. "Most interesting, these native names—I wish one knew more about them."

"They're outlandish, if you ask me," said Mrs. Peachey, giving Robin an extra spoonful of cream out of pity for his perilous future. "Why don't they give the towns good sensible English names, as they used to in Governor Macquarie's day? Although I must say he was a bit too fond of calling everything after himself or his wife."

Cassie tried hard to be present during the interview between Missabella and Mr. Rose, but had to be content with lingering on the front porch to watch him depart.

"They've been talking for at least an hour," she reported to Francis. "I do hope Missabella will tell us what it was all about. He's a rich-looking gentleman, isn't he?"

At dinner Missabella appeared to be in good spirits. She had, in fact, been rather withdrawn and anxious for the past few days, for, as she wrote to her brother Hugh: "These children rely on me so absolutely, and I undertook so confidently to improve their condition by bringing them here. Everything is so strange and disordered in this new land that I can only pray that my single powers of organization will prove sufficient to meet all emergencies." This morning her prayers had been answered, at least in part, by the arrival of Mr. Rose, who had provided much useful advice as well as offers of practical help.

"He suggests that we travel by coach as far as Appin, which will mean that about half of our journey will be made in fair comfort. Then he will lend us a dray and a guide to take us to the Illawarra, as apparently the track is very steep and difficult in places. Also, he can sell us a good Jersey cow in calf, and a work-horse. He believes that the country round the Five Islands is good for raising dairy cattle, and our property is not far south of there."

"Wasn't it lucky that I met him!" said Paul, beaming. "He's just like a fairy godfather, isn't he?"

"It has proved lucky in another respect, too," said Missabella, turning to Francis. "Mr. Rose is on the governing board of the Free Grammar School, and is going to try to obtain a place for you. He is to let me know in the next few days if he has been successful, and then you shall have to go for an interview with Dr. Halloran, the headmaster."

Francis, who had been thinking longingly of the Jersey cow and the draft-horse, managed a faint smile of gratitude, and concentrated on his mutton stew.

"Mr. Rose has a finger in a great many pies in the Colony," observed Mrs. Peachey, bearing to the table an enormous apple-pudding. "And to think he came here in irons!"

Missabella paused in the act of offering Sally-Lou a final forkful of boiled potato.

"You mean, he was a convict? A *criminal?*"

"We didn't think of all of them like that, Ma'am," said Mrs. Peachey, with an offended dignity which made Missabella wonder suddenly what the late Mr. Peachey's record had been. "Once they got their pardons, you didn't ask what they'd done in the first place. It must be nearly thirty years since Mr. Rose was sent out, and he's never looked back."

As the children were listening to this exchange with the keenest absorption, Missabella decided to try another subject.

"As soon as we have seen Francis settled at school, we shall be on our way. I understand that April and May are often the best months of the year here, and there will be a great deal of work to do before winter starts."

"I'm told it's a fine school Dr. Halloran has," said Mrs. Peachey, who by now knew every detail of the orphans' affairs. "He'll turn you into a regular young gentleman, Francis, with all that grammar and versifying and such. He writes poetry himself, they say. And," she added in a low aside to Missabella, "you won't be wanting to look too closely at *his* credentials, either."

"Come, children," said Missabella, rising and casting a quelling glance in her landlady's direction. "It's time for you younger ones to rest."

There was little rest in the week that followed for any orphan over the age of nine. As necessities were acquired, through purchase or gift—Mrs. Peachey turned out her many cupboards and pressed upon Missabella a variety of articles both useful and otherwise—they were stowed in hessian bags in the hallway outside Missabella's room, to the inconvenience of passers-by. Once again the orphans' clothes were sorted and patched and altered and aired, and day after day Selina was busy with her needle. One of Missabella's bargains, discovered in a store in Pitt Street, was a length of tough cotton material striped in blue and white; with the combined assistance of Selina, Mrs. Peachey and Susannah, this was cut and sewed into shirts for the two smallest boys, and loose, shapeless, but quite practical dresses for all the girls.

"We shall look like a party from the work-house," sighed Selina, thinking wistfully of the dainty lawns and muslins her mother had left her, fabrics which had not stood up too well to the rigors of the voyage, and were destined to be made over for Sally-Lou.

"They're just the right clothes for milking the cows in," said Cassie. "When we reach Appin, I'm to learn how to milk *and* churn butter. And both Gavin and Luke will have to practice shooting, in case we're attacked by blacks."

But Selina was accustomed to Cassie's taunts by this time, and merely bent her sleek head again over her sewing.

It was the outfitting of Francis which gave Missabella the greatest concern. The boy was growing tall, and could hardly appear at a school for young colonial gentlemen in sadly outgrown jacket and trousers. When Mr. Rose sent word that Francis was to go next morning to be interviewed by Dr. Halloran, Missabella in desperation took out the money that she had set aside for emergencies, and bought him a new pair of trousers, a pair of white shirts, and a smart blue jacket with brass buttons. Mrs. Peachey unearthed a peaked cap that had belonged to her husband, and in all this finery Francis was pronounced very elegant by the other children, who gathered to wish him well before he set out for Phillip Street and the Grammar School.

"And remember," Missabella counseled him as they walked along Chapel Row, "you have had a good elementary education, and have absolutely nothing to be ashamed of. Never forget that your father was a hero of Waterloo."

As Francis confessed later to Cassie, he had been tempted to give a really poor account of himself at the interview, and to offer the wrong answers to the fairly simple examination questions set for him. If he failed, then Missabella would have no alternative but to let him go south with the others.

"But I just couldn't do it," he said sadly. "Missabella was so sure I would do well, and then Dr. Halloran sat there looking so stern, in a black gown. He has the kind of eyes that see right through you."

"It's a pity he didn't see everything, and then he'd have known you didn't want to go to his old school," remarked Cassie. "Do you think you passed?"

"I suppose so. Missabella signed some papers, and the Doctor said he would see me next Monday morning at eight o'clock. There are two hours for dinner in the middle of the day, and school again till five."

"Oh, I wish if anyone had to go to school, it could be me!" cried Cassie. "I'd much rather work at a place like the Grammar School, and study history and Latin and geography, than learn how to sew and cook. I know Missabella will never have time to keep up my French lessons, but she will always make me do my sewing."

"You would have liked the Doctor's study," said Francis. "It was full of books, hundreds of them. They'll be wasted on me."

"You must write often, and tell me what you're learning," Cassie urged.

"I might, if you write to *me*. I'll want to know exactly

what the farm is like, and how many animals you buy, and what you plant. You see, I shan't have any holidays until Christmas—Missabella explained she couldn't afford the money for me to travel more than once a year."

Brother and sister stared at each other as the full meaning of these words dawned upon them. Christmas was nine months away, and Chapel Row and the Illawarra as far apart as earth and stars, when there were no funds available for the journey between. For the first time Cassie began to understand how isolated she and her fellow-orphans were going to be, and with this thought came the glimmering of an understanding of Missabella's tremendous and lonely responsibility.

"Oh, Francis, I do wish you were coming! Not just because I'll miss you, but because I don't think any of the rest of us has enough sense to be a real help to Missabella!"

 6

The Eleventh Orphan

O N THEIR LAST Sunday morning in Sydney, the children were allowed a rare and delightful treat. As they filed in at Mrs. Peachey's gate after attending morning service at near-by St. James's Church, Missabella announced:

"I think Francis deserves some kind of farewell celebration, and as it's such a fine day, I shall let you take some food in a basket, and have it out of doors. I believe I can trust you and Gavin, Francis, to take care of the others, and not to lead them into any unsuitable places. Somewhere on or near the 'Racecourse' would be quite pleasant."

Jubilant, the children ran to change from their Sunday clothes. Selina thought at first that she might stay behind quietly with her sewing, but the day was altogether too clear and fresh and inviting to be wasted indoors. So she joined the others in time to see them receiving a large laden basket from Mrs. Peachey, who had been warned of the outing well in advance.

"You'll find plenty for everybody, and don't let Paul stuff himself," she said, with a wink for her favorite. Of all the orphans, Paul was the one who most appreciated good food.

As the children hurried up the hill, a few carriages were still drawing away from the church, and others of the congregation were strolling through Hyde Park, often known as the Racecourse, although it was no longer used as such. The children knew this large open area quite well, for it was here that they usually took their supervised walks, and Cassie, for one, preferred new pastures.

"Let's go on," she suggested. "There must be lots of more interesting places. We shan't get lost, as long as we can still see the church spire."

"Missabella said not to go anywhere unsuitable," Selina primly reminded her.

"She only meant those noisy parts like the Rocks and Bunker's Hill," declared Cassie, who had studied Sydney's topography fairly thoroughly during her outings with Missabella. "Out here it's as quiet as could be."

They had crossed the park and were standing at the top of a hill, facing east. Certainly the prospect before them was more enticing than the one behind. On their left the green waters of Wolomoloo Bay glinted in the sun, lapping the rocks of Mrs. Macquarie's Point. Below them a bright little stream ran down to join the bay; on the other side of it a large house stood in several acres of garden, with a steep sand-hill beyond.

"There doesn't seem to be any path," said Francis doubtfully.

"We'll go and find out," was Cassie's answer, and she forthwith led the not unwilling party down the slope to the stream. Here, fortunately, there were stepping-stones, and if a few shoes became a little damp, no one cared, for the sun was warm enough to dry them. Most important, the basket was maneuvered across without mishap, and everyone set out happily for the harbor shore. A brief search showed them the ideal spot for an outdoor meal—a flat rock backed by a tall cliff which sheltered them from the nor'-easterly breeze, yet provided an excellent view over the water to the scrub-covered bluffs on the other side of the harbor.

"Now let's see what's for dinner," urged Paul.

Mrs. Peachey was a good judge of the extent of youthful appetites. The apparently bottomless basket yielded cold pasties, liberally stuffed with chopped mutton and potatoes, slices of currant cake, hunks of cheese, and a plentiful supply of apples. The only member of the party who did not do justice to all this was Francis, whose thoughts tended to drift unbidden towards the morrow.

"You'll be the lucky one, Francis," said Marianne, who was not the most tactful of girls. "You'll be eating Mrs. Peachey's dinners for weeks and weeks."

"While we live on fish and wild berries and roots," added Paul cheerfully.

"I haven't seen many berries, even," remarked Martha. "What do the black people eat?"

"Grubs and snakes," replied Cassie, who had been avidly studying the twice-weekly issues of the *Gazette*. "And those queer jumping animals."

"Kangaroos," supplied Francis glumly.

"I wish we could see one," said Paul. "Susannah's gentleman-friend says they're six feet tall at least, and jump yards in the air."

"If you mean that man with a beard, the one who sits on Mrs. Peachey's porch step, then you can't believe anything he says," declared Cassie. "He told me he'd seen an animal with fur and webbed feet, that swims and lays eggs. I never heard anything so silly."

"He could be right," protested Luke. "He goes all over the country, cutting timber. He knows the Illawarra, because he went by boat to a place called Kiarmi, and he says there are trees like cabbages on a long, long stalk."

"We'll find out for ourselves, soon enough," said Gavin, and then they were all silent for a moment, remembering Francis.

"Come on, let's pack up and go for a walk," said Cassie, rising with a most unladylike display of ankle. "We have time to go all the way round to Farm Cove."

As Cassie had by far the soundest knowledge of the lie of the land, the others did not question this statement. Soon they were all scrambling over the rocks below Mrs. Macquarie's Walk, with the harbor water lapping in little soft waves beside them. Cassie, as usual, hurried ahead, closely followed by Luke and Paul, with Gavin and Francis in preoccupied silence a few yards behind. Selina and the twins were looking for shells, so no one noticed when Robin and Sally-Lou dropped back. It was not until all the others had rounded the bluff, and were facing across Farm Cove to Bennelong Point, that Francis, at least, recalled his responsibilities.

"Hadn't we better go back and find them?" he asked. "Sally-Lou might slip on the rocks."

"I think they're coming now," said Selina. "I can see Sally-Lou's pink sunbonnet."

The sunbonnet was indeed bobbing with even more than accustomed liveliness, and Robin was having difficulty in keeping up with its wearer. Beyond them, and traveling much more slowly and warily, was a third figure, strange enough to draw startled exclamations from the waiting children.

"Gracious, it's a black boy!" cried Selina.

"He's got a spear," added Paul. "And hardly anything on."

"Should we call for help?" demanded Martha, looking upwards to see if any couples were taking a Sunday afternoon promenade around Mrs. Macquarie's Walk.

"Of course not," said Cassie scornfully. "He's not much bigger than Robin, and there are ten of *us*. He's probably been using his spear to catch fish."

Sally-Lou and Robin now rejoined the party, the former chattering excitedly of their encounter.

"He was behind a rock, watching us," she explained. "Robin was frightened, but I wasn't, because the black boy put his spear down. I told him to come with us."

"He wouldn't understand, anyway," said Francis, with some relief, for he could well envisage Missabella's consternation if Sally-Lou brought a half-naked black child home to tea. "He might live in a hut somewhere near."

The stranger meanwhile stood at a safe distance and watched the English children with evident interest. He could have been any age between six and twelve, although the fact that he was carrying a spear with some confidence suggested that he might be nearer Luke's age than Robin's. His one garment was a ragged pair of trousers, originally of European make, which hung halfway down his spindly legs. So black was his face that when he finally opened his mouth in a broad grin, the white of his teeth looked positively unnatural.

"He seems friendly, anyway," observed Cassie, her ready curiosity aroused. "Let's try talking to him."

She essayed a combination of simple English and sign-language, but the boy merely continued to smile, giving no other indication that he had understood. At last Francis, with a glance at the sun now declining behind the Dawes Point garrison, urged Cassie to give up her attempts and proceed homewards to Chapel Row. The others straggled off around Farm Cove, and Cassie was soon occupied with leading Sally-Lou, who had suddenly discovered she was too tired to walk unaided. They had reached the top of the hill and were about to turn down into Bent Street, when Cassie looked back and saw that Robin, in the rear of the procession, was being followed at a distance of a few yards by his new black friend.

"Tell him to go home, Cassie," said Francis. "Surely he'll know what that means."

But the boy remained impassive, and nothing Francis or Gavin could do in the way of frightening him off had any effect. He just retreated a pace or two, then set out again in Robin's footsteps.

"Well, he can't come into Mrs. Peachey's house, so he'll *have* to go home when we get there," said Cassie. "Or do you suppose he mightn't have a home?"

"We can't help it, anyway," Francis declared. "Or are you going to ask Missabella to look after him as well as all of us?"

But even Cassie saw the impossibility of such a suggestion.

About half-way down Bent Street stood a large stone fountain, and here the children paused to quench their thirst before entering Chapel Row. A number of townsfolk were gathered here, spending the fine mellow evening in talk, or drawing the clear cool water. One of the loungers was Susannah's gentleman-friend, the cedar-cutter with the black beard.

"Out for a bit of fresh air, are you?" he remarked cheerfully. "And then back to Mrs. Peachey's supper. Wish I had your luck. I see you've got an extra mouth to feed, too."

He indicated the native boy, who hung back in the shadow of a porch-roof.

"He won't go away," said Cassie. Despite his wild tales of furry duck-billed mammals, she liked Susannah's Harry. "Do you know where he comes from?"

One of Harry's companions stepped forward to peer more closely at the small dark figure with the spear.

"They all look the same to me," he said. "But it could be the one they call Cammy. The folk round here call him that, because he's supposed to have come from some tribe across the harbor, with a name like Cammeraygal. Sounds real heathenish, don't it?"

"Does he have a family, then?" asked Francis.

The man shrugged.

"Dunno. He's been hanging about Sydney Cove and the Rocks for a few months. Never seems to have anyone with him."

"Perhaps he's an orphan like us," ventured Paul, with some sympathy. "But he's lucky he knows how to catch his own dinner."

"We must go home, and if he follows us, he'll just have to sleep in the street," Francis declared, feeling he had enough troubles already, without adding to them the responsibility of a dispossessed aborigine. After all, creatures like Cammy were by no means rare in Sydney Town; separated from their scattering tribes, a number of natives took up their abode on the fringes of the settlement, where they lived a sort of shadowy half-life, neither accepted by the newcomers nor comforted by their ancient tribal rites and loyalties. Probably the most unusual thing about Cammy was the fact that he was a child on his own, for the families mostly stayed together, wherever they were.

When the children arrived at Mrs. Peachey's gate, Cammy withdrew to the opposite side of the street, and watched them go into the house. Robin may not have understood much of the conversation at the fountain, but he felt instinctively that Cammy regarded him as a friend, and as the others trooped into the hallway, Robin ran back to Cammy with an apple that had somehow been left in the lunch basket. This gift was received with suitable gravity, briefly inspected, and stowed in Cammy's trousers pocket.

Ten minutes later, when Missabella had heard the story and glanced from the front window to see the central figure of it, Cammy had gone. Missabella and most of her charges were quite relieved, but Robin and Paul continued to peep out at the street at intervals during the evening. It was the thought of the spear that fascinated Paul; Robin, however, had stored in his slow mind the memory of a wide, white, and friendly smile.

***

The next morning nobody in Missabella's party had much time to think of Cammy at all. At a quarter to eight Francis set out for school, very neat and handsome in his new clothes, but with feet that dragged every yard of the way to Dr. Halloran's door. At noon he would eat his last meal— for many months, at least— with his sister and brother and friends; they were taking the afternoon coach from Brickfield Hill. He had been up since five, helping to sew the sacks of provisions, sitting on the lid of the trunks to make them shut, and rolling up bedding. It would need an entire coach, he reflected sadly, to hold all the orphans and their worldly goods. If only they would find one corner for him!

Later in the morning Missabella and Gavin went to the convict-barracks to collect the convict assigned to the former as her laborer. As Gavin told Cassie afterwards, it was rather like picking up a parcel from a store.

"Missabella signed a paper, agreeing to give the fellow food and lodging, and then he was brought out and told to follow us here. He isn't in irons or anything, but he doesn't look dangerous, does he?"

Cassie contemplated the figure on the steps of the back porch, and thought that "dangerous" was certainly the most unlikely adjective to describe him. He was decked out in new regulation-clothing from the Government stores— duck trousers, ill-cut woollen jacket and grey waistcoat, wool cap and worsted stockings. A neckerchief was partly visible beneath a short fair beard. As he was very slight of build, his clothes hung loosely upon him, and his narrow shoulders seemed to droop under the weight of his jacket.

"He doesn't look strong enough to chop down trees and put up fences," said Cassie doubtfully. "Perhaps he was ill during the voyage out. What is his name?"

"I saw it on the paper," answered Gavin. "It's Ebenezer Bancroft, and he's twenty-two. Missabella wouldn't let me see any more."

Missabella hardly considered it proper that a twelve-year-old boy should know the details of any convict's sentence, but privately she had been quite startled to learn that Ebenezer had been given transportation for ten years for pawning an article of clothing belonging to the printer for whom he had worked; the theft had taken place, she noticed, in a large town not far from her own Switherby, and remembering the misery of some of those hunger-haunted streets, she was inclined to think that the judge's sentence had been more than a little harsh. However, the fact remained that Ebenezer was a convicted criminal in the eyes of society, and as such must be kept apart from such impressionable creatures as growing children. Only—*how* were they to be kept apart when they were all confined to the same small patch of land in the middle of the bush?

At dinner-time Ebenezer ate in the kitchen, and Susannah reported that he seemed "ever such a decent young chap, and quiet as a mouse." He was not the only person to eat the midday meal in silence. A sudden pall of gloom had fallen upon almost all the orphans, as they realized how very soon they would be leaving the comfort and security of Mrs. Peachey's lodging-house.

"Tell us about your morning at school, Francis," urged Missabella. "Did you start on your Latin?"

"Yes, Ma'am. It was quite interesting, thank you," said Francis dutifully. "And Mr. Rose called on the Doctor to see how I was getting on. Mr. Rose was on his way back to Appin."

"He will be there before us, then," remarked Cassie. "We have to leave the coach at Parramatta and go on by cart. Mr. Rose has his own carriage—I've seen it."

"Susannah says there was a little black fellow hanging around the gate this morning," said Mrs. Peachey. "She sent him off quick enough, but he seemed to want to know something. He kept looking at your luggage on the front porch. Susannah thought he might try and steal something."

"Cammy wouldn't steal," said Paul indignantly.

"How do you know it was Cammy?" asked Gavin. "And what's more, how do you know he wouldn't take things?"

Paul being unable to answer either question, the meal was concluded in silence. Cassie should have gone to tidy up for the journey, but she slipped into the hall with Francis.

"Will you write down the Latin you learnt this morning? And look, I've made you a present."

She produced a square of fine lawn, laboriously and unskilfully hemmed into the semblance of a handkerchief. Knowing how his sister loathed sewing, Francis took it with real gratitude, and in return wrote out the present tense of "Amare: To love".

"That's all we've done, so far. Cassie—you will remember to write, won't you?"

"Of course I'll remember. But Missabella says the postal service will be unreliable."

They stood awkwardly in the dark hall, and for a moment the family resemblance between them was strong.

"Don't worry about Paul," said Cassie. "I'll look after him. It seems a long time since we were all together in Switherby, doesn't it? I think Paul's quite forgotten it."

"Do you wish you were back there?" asked Francis.

"No, not a bit. I hate going away from you, but I can't help feeling glad about the farm and the traveling and all the adventure. If I were back in Switherby, I should have to try and be a lady all my life. In the Illawarra I won't need to bother much."

Francis gazed at her thin, bright-eyed, determined face, her shaggy hair and unbecoming clothes—she was wearing the striped smock-like dress and black worsted stockings— and was glad that she at least was unlikely to change.

"I had better go back to school. I've said good-bye to Missabella, and I'd rather not say anything to the others, not even Paul. He's so excited about the journey."

Cassie nodded agreement, and turned away. She would brush her hair, shine her shoes, sweep the back porch—do anything positive and active, in fact, to stop her from thinking of Francis on his solitary way to the Grammar School.

As it happened, however, Francis was not alone for the first part of the short walk. Selina had been waiting for him, and asked shyly if she might keep him company to the corner of Chapel Row and Hunter Street.

"Missabella asked me to buy something she had forgotten, and I don't like to walk here alone. I wish you could come to the Illawarra with us, Francis."

"You don't wish it as much as I do," said Francis, then, feeling he must sound ungracious, he added, "I shall miss all of you very much."

"Some day you'll be a fine gentleman," Selina said wistfully. "And we shall be still working away out in the woods—"

"They call it the bush," Francis reminded her.

"I don't much care what they call it. I shall hate it. And I'm afraid of the black people and the snakes and spiders, and the being so many miles from other people."

Francis glanced at her, and saw that her distress was real enough. He had to admit that she was a very delicate-looking candidate for a life of pioneering; she had put on her old pink muslin frock, and wore her lace mittens and a white bonnet. But Francis dimly understood that this was her own particular brand of courage—to set forth into the wilderness dressed in her dainty best, and to remember that wherever she was she remained a squire's grand-daughter. Cassie would have snorted and derided, while Francis could find it in his heart to hope that the unknown and distant Illawarra would not deal too harshly with Selina and her little lace mittens. After he had parted from her at the corner, he climbed the hill very slowly, and looked back often to catch a glimpse of the pink-clad figure with the trailing silvery hair.

7

The Illawarra Shore

"YOU'LL NOT GET a dray down that track, and that's the truth," said Mick Phelan. "Last fellow that tried it was run over by 'is own cart."

"Is there no other road?" asked Missabella unbelievingly.

"Folks in the Illawarra mostly make their own roads, Ma'am. Four or five years ago, you'd 'ave 'ad to go by Bull-Eye, an' been much worse off."

Missabella frowned. By all the standards of her upbringing, this grey-bearded old farm-hand was intolerably disrespectful, but it seemed that she was to be entirely dependent on him for the next day or two. Phelan was the guide that Mr. Rose had offered her for the journey to her holding; it appeared that he knew the district better than any man in the Campbelltown area. He had hardly glanced at Missabella's map—in any case he was unable to read—but from her description he could tell almost exactly where her grant would be in relation to the Five Islands, the closest semblance of a settlement. Under Mr. Rose's instructions he would stay with the party long enough to mark out the boundaries.

"Then how *are* we to travel?" demanded Missabella,

thinking of the mound of luggage now stored in the Mount Gilead barn, of the sleek Jersey cow due to calve in a few days, and, most important of all, nine weary children aged from five to twelve.

"Pack-'orses. You can take a cart to the top of the mountain, an' go the rest of the way on foot. 'Ave to be careful of the cow, though—she's a val'i'ble animal."

Missabella did indeed suspect that Mr. Rose had charged her only a part of the cow's real worth, for a fine beast like Jessie would be greatly prized in the Colony. The horse, too, though elderly and shaggy, was a considerable bargain. The children were even now taking in turns to ride round the paddocks on his safe broad back, and Tomkins, quite unused to such treatment, was nevertheless accepting it with complete amiability.

"You'll need to borrow a couple more 'orses," Phelan went on. "Mr. Rose'll trust me to bring 'em back. That convict feller doesn't look much good at hard work—pity they didn't give you a bigger chap."

Again, Missabella had to admit to herself that Phelan was right. Eben, as the children had named him, was willing and docile and unlikely to offer any insolence whatsoever, but his physical capacity was sadly low.

"We shall have to manage as best we can," said Missabella. "Mr. Rose thinks we should start out early tomorrow."

"That's right," agreed Phelan. "Could be a change comin' in the weather. River's impossible to cross after a few inches of rain."

To Missabella, this was simply one more good reason for making their departure as speedy as possible. The Rose family were being wonderfully kind and hospitable; they had insisted on giving two bedrooms over to Missabella and the girls, while the boys slept in the barn, and provided all sorts of additions to the provisions the party had brought with them. But Missabella was worried by her hosts' generosity; she had been in the Colony long enough to realize that every landholder was waging a constant struggle to survive, and she had no hope of repaying the Roses' kindness for a long time to come. Also, the longer she stayed at Mount Gilead, the more reluctant the children would be to set out for their own grant—all of them loved the Roses' farm, with its rolling paddocks and great spreading gum-trees and abundance of livestock. Mr. Rose was even building a dam, a fascinating novelty to the younger children, who were in a continuous state of muddy dampness.

"I wish we could stay here for always," mourned Sally-Lou, on the last night. "Will our own farm be like this, Cassie?"

"Not a bit," firmly answered Cassie, the only child among them to look forward to the next stage of the journey. "We shall have to *make* it, you see. But we'll still have Jessie and her calf, and Tomkins."

There was one more live addition to the group, however. After breakfast next morning, Mr. Rose brought in a sack that appeared to be in a curious state of upheaval.

"A farewell present for Sally-Lou," he announced. "But I would advise you to keep it in the sack while you're traveling."

It was a half-grown tortoise-shell cat, wild-eyed and offended by its imprisonment, but quickly placated by a lump of butter from the breakfast-table. Sally-Lou, greatly delighted, at once called her pet "Rosie," after her host—a further insult to the cat, who was in fact a male.

"Now all you need is a dog," said Mr. Rose. "If you visit

us in a month or so, we might have a puppy for you, but I'm afraid you'll all be much too busy to go visiting."

"Don't forget we have some butter and milk for you to take," added his wife. "You'll have none of your own until the calf is born. I've wrapped the butter in a damp cloth to keep it fresh, and the milk is in a stone jar. No, don't bother returning it—you'll need it yourselves."

Missabella, who had spent some time in the Mount Gilead dairy learning how to set milk and make butter, was grateful once again for Mr. Rose's help. Yesterday Eben had made a clumsy but workable churn, and Gavin, Luke and Cassie had all taken lessons in milking.

"This is much better than learning how to spell," said Luke. "I'm going to have first turn at milking our own cow after the calf is born."

"You and Gavin and Eben can have *all* the turns," vowed Cassie. "I just don't like being so close to cows. I shall look after the horse."

When the time came for departure, however, Cassie was disgusted to find that she was to make the initial stage of the journey on the dray, with the other girls.

"There will be a great deal of walking to do later," Missabella said firmly. "Besides, I need you up there to help keep the baggage steady. Martha and Marianne, please see that Sally-Lou's kitten stays in the sack, and don't let Sally lean over the side."

The procession assembling in the Mount Gilead stable-yard was indeed remarkable. Two of Mr. Rose's sturdiest horses were harnessed to the big unwieldy dray, on which the five girls were perched among the various odd-shaped articles of luggage. The twins were carefully nursing milk, butter, and eggs, while Cassie held the butter-churn and

Sally-Lou the sack containing a wildly agitated Rosie. Selina had the prize position, beside Phelan, the driver, but even she had to guard a bag full of tools between her feet.

"Look at that lucky Gavin!" said Cassie enviously, as Tomkins lumbered up with Gavin on his back, and the musket slung to the saddle. Eben came across the yard with a sack of flour, which he hoisted on to Tomkins behind his rider. The flour had been ground at Mr. Rose's own mill, but Missabella had insisted on paying for this service, like all the other settlers in the district.

"I'm afraid there'll be no mill any closer to you than ours," Mr. Rose observed. "Forty or so miles are a lot to cover to get your wheat ground. But remember—if you're ever in need at all, send Eben or one of the boys up to us. You won't find many neighbors around the Five Islands."

"You're very kind," said Missabella, for the last time. She had donned her best traveling outfit, despite the promised warmth of the April day, and managed to maintain her dignified deportment even as she took her place beside Selina.

" 'Ope you've got some canvas 'andy," said Phelan. "There'll be some rain before the day's out. 'Ear them kookaburras?"

Certainly several jackasses were making considerable noise at the top of a blue-gum near the gate, but whether as a prophecy of changing weather or out of sheer amusement at the cavalcade below, the children did not know. Eben had now led Jessie the cow to join Tomkins, and behind pranced Luke, Paul and Robin, all in great excitement.

"Tell them boys to be quiet," ordered Phelan, who seemed to have taken complete charge of the party. "Do they want to scare that cow out of 'er wits?"

"They will have to ride on the dray before long," said

Missabella, wondering at her own subservience to this disrespectful old man. "They will soon get tired. Eben is to see to the cow."

Eben and Jessie had developed a sort of mutual understanding and affection—Cassie had even noticed the convict whispering in the animal's ear when he thought he was unobserved. To the humans around him he hardly spoke at all, beyond answering Missabella's commands, although the overtures of the younger children met with a tentative smile and nod.

The sun was climbing from a bank of heavy bluish cloud and peeping over the stable-roof as Mr. Rose gave the order to depart. Phelan uttered a startling sound, a kind of hoarse bellowed "Geddup!" and the wheels of the dray creaked into motion. There was a chorus of "Good-byes" from the children, and a response of "Good luck!" from the Roses, and then the dray was swaying along the rutted track through the paddocks.

"Good luck, eh!" said Phelan. "I've no doubt you'll need it, with all them young 'uns to feed. Mind you don't let them stray too far, neither—most o' the Illawarra is like a jungle, easy to get lost in."

"What about the blacks? Are they troublesome?" asked Missabella, keeping her voice low for the sake of the children behind her, though Selina listened with a horrified fascination.

"Just depends," replied Phelan judicially. "Sometimes they sneak about at night, stealin' cattle an' spoilin' the crops. But what damages the crops most is the cockatoos."

"What are they?" demanded Cassie, who had edged her way forward.

"Birds, Miss. Mind, they're pretty critters, red an' blue

an' green. The Illawarra's full of birds, all kinds of 'em. You'd never see their like back 'ome. An' there's plenty of fish in the sea an' the rivers, an' a tree called the cabbage-palm with leaves you can make 'ats an' baskets of."

"It sounds wonderful," said Cassie, wishing suddenly that Francis were here to share her excitement. Selina was still trying to be ladylike, sheltering her complexion from the strengthening sun and shuddering at the mention of blacks and cockatoos, and the twins were too stolid to respond to Cassie's expressions of delight. With a sigh, Cassie dangled her legs over the edge of the dray—Missabella's back was turned—and gazed dreamily upwards at the thickening canopy of silvery-green leaves. There was no way of measuring the passage of the hours, for every stretch of bushland resembled the last, and they were in almost perpetual shade.

The horses plodded on slowly but surely enough, for on this part of the journey their path was fairly well defined. The smaller boys scrambled up on to the dray; Sally-Lou handed her sack to Marianne, and fell asleep with her head on a roll of bedding.

At last it was Cassie's turn to ride Tomkins, and instantly she felt alive again, though the old horse's pace was far from frisky. She allowed him to fall back to the end of the procession, and now and then she let herself lose sight of the others altogether, so she could pretend that she was truly lost in this vast forest of black-butted gums and tough scrub. Presently she became a trifle uneasy, for while she could still hear the creak of the dray and the thudding of hooves on sandy ground, she was nonetheless only too conscious of the immense loneliness on either side of the track.

"Geddup, Tomkins," she urged, imitating Phelan's admonition.

Tomkins' reaction was quite startling. He shied violently and then swivelled round to point his nose towards home. What had produced this eccentric behavior, however, was not Cassie's command, but the sudden appearance on the track of a half-naked figure with a spear.

Cassie opened her mouth to shriek for help, and stopped herself in time. Terror had made the apparition twice its actual size at first; now she perceived that it was smaller than herself, and moreover, dimly familiar.

The boy indicated by putting down his spear that his intentions were peaceful. Cassie nodded to show she understood, and said tentatively:

"Are you Cammy?"

At this the boy grinned widely, and patted himself on the chest.

"But however did you get here?" asked Cassie, meanwhile soothing the suspicious Tomkins. She went on more slowly, with gestures in the direction of what she hoped was Sydney, "You walked? From there?"

Again Cammy nodded, and bent down to show the marks of the wheels in the dirt.

"You followed us? All the way? But what for?"

Cammy hesitated, frowned, then went on a few paces simulating a limp, with such exaggeration that the quick-witted Cassie at once understood.

"You're looking for Robin? Rob-in," she repeated, and Cammy spoke for the first time, trying out the name several times. Finally he pointed to Cassie.

"I'm Cassie Brown—Cassie. It sounds a bit like Cammy, only you hiss like a snake in the middle."

She hissed dramatically, enjoying this queer one-sided conversation. Cammy seemed pleased, too, and with a great effort pronounced her name.

"We're going to the Illawarra, near the sea," Cassie continued, and was trying to illustrate "sea" when a call from the track ahead startled them both. Cammy darted behind a rock, and gestured Cassie to go on.

"All right. I won't tell anyone. I expect you can look after yourself here better than we can."

Hurrying to join the rest of the group, she wondered if Cammy intended to stay with them permanently. He was certainly a long way from his own people, if indeed he had any. And how would Missabella receive him? Would she insist on sending him away?

"She couldn't *make* him go," Cassie argued with herself. "And he could be quite useful, knowing how to catch fish and everything."

When she came up with the others, she found that Phelan was preparing to lead them across a river, presumably the stream which he had hoped would not be in flood. This morning it was low enough to ford, though fairly fast-flowing, and the only member of the party to object to crossing it was poor Jessie, who had to be coaxed by Eben every yard of the way.

"We'd best stop for a bite o' something now, then get on to the top o' the mountain before mid-afternoon," said Phelan. "It'll take us an hour at least to get down."

"Shall we be at our holding by nightfall, then?" asked Missabella anxiously.

Phelan glanced at what was visible of the sky between the trees.

"We'll try, but there's no tellin'. Rain might slow us down, Ma'am, an' then we'll 'ave to camp somewhere for the night."

"I suppose," said Missabella philosophically, "that we

should be camping in any case, whether we reach our land or not. It will take a little time to put up even the roughest shelter."

Phelan looked rather pained.

"Beggin' yer pardon, Ma'am, but first things first. What we've got to do right off is make a pen for the cow—lose 'er, an' you might as well all go 'ome."

A little reflection showed the surprised Missabella that Phelan was right once again—was not the long-suffering Jessie to provide milk and butter and cheese, and in the long run perhaps the party's very livelihood?

So they struggled on as fast as they could, with Phelan occasionally forgetting the company and cursing his horses in fluent language that made Selina blush. Missabella no longer cared, which revealed just how anxious she was that the journey should be rapidly and safely accomplished. Some time after noon the track became steeper and more diffi-cult; Phelan slowed the horses to a walk, and waited for the rest of the group to catch up. When Cassie arrived on Tomkins' back—it was her turn once more—she found the dray halted in a slight clearing, and Phelan ordering the others to help unload.

"Can't the dray go any further?" Missabella asked, peer-ing at the screen of trees ahead.

"Come and see!" cried Paul from somewhere beyond. "We're on the edge of the world!"

Cassie dismounted and led Tomkins through the trees. It was as well that she progressed with more than her usual caution, for quite suddenly the trees vanished, and the ground opened at her feet. She was gazing down a long, thickly overgrown mountainside so steep that it seemed al-most a precipice. Far below, so far that she drew in her breath in disbelief, light-green patches among the prevailing dark foliage showed the presence of the cabbage-palms Phelan had described; she let her glance travel slowly away from them until she saw the pale-gold arcs of sand and the white foam, and then the immense deep blue of the sea. A faint sound came to her on the still air, the sigh of waves along mile upon mile of coastline where no trace of human habitation was visible.

Paul was jumping up and down in excitement, but Robin, beside him, drew back in awed astonishment and clutched at Cassie's hand.

"Doesn't the sea look lovely when you don't have to watch it from a ship!" said Paul. "Is our farm somewhere down there, Cassie? There's nothing but trees."

Behind him Phelan gave a grunt that might have indicated amusement. He had come to show Missabella the way they must follow.

"An' that's just what your farm will be—acres of trees, all waitin' to be chopped down. You see that long point yonder— we 'ave to get a few miles past that to reach your place."

Cassie looked southward as he pointed, noticing the five small islands that gave the near-by district its name, and the lagoon called "Tom Thumb's" after the boat of the explorer Bass; beyond these a succession of beaches and bluff-shaped headlands culminated in a long low spur of land like a giant finger. While the shoreline was clearly defined, and the cliffs relatively free of scrub, the countryside immediately behind them was a dense, apparently trackless mass of jungly growth.

Missabella was silent for a few minutes. Perhaps her thoughts returned to the neat, orderly, closely-settled lands around Switherby, and boggled completely at the primitive vastness below her. However, she knew what had to be done.

"Back to work, everyone," she commanded briskly. "All our baggage has to be loaded on to the horses."

The younger children were stricken with horror at the weight the three horses were to carry. With the aid of ropes and straps and cunning contrivance, Phelan loaded the animals so that their burdens were as evenly balanced as possible, and still secure.

"Poor old Tomkins will never be able to carry all that," protested Paul.

"Mebbe you'll carry it instead, then," was Phelan's only response, and Paul retreated to the end of the line, where Missabella was handing out various portable bundles to the older children.

"Not you, Gavin—you're to help Phelan lead the horses. And you small children keep close behind me, and watch where you're putting your feet. Martha, take that sack from Sally-Lou—she will need to have both her hands free."

In less than ten minutes the children knew the reason for Missabella's cautioning. The track, barely wide enough to allow the passage of the horses' packs, was from the beginning so steeply angled that the animals frequently slid on their haunches, and it seemed hardly short of miraculous that Phelan could prevent the leader from pulling the entire baggage train to destruction. In places the ground was damp from hidden springs, or studded with mossy rocks that threatened the equilibrium of humans and horses alike, to say nothing of one terrified cow. But Eben exerted every scrap of strength he possessed to check Jessie when her progress became too rapid for safety; Cassie, coming down behind him at the head of the band of children, was filled with admiration for his tenacity.

"It's as well Jessie hasn't had her calf yet," she panted. "We should have had to carry it. Now I see why we couldn't bring the dray any farther."

"It's horrible," groaned Selina, catching at a tree-trunk to steady herself. "Why couldn't we have stayed in Sydney? I'm sure I saw a black man just now, when I looked back."

Cassie smiled to herself, thinking of Cammy. He would probably have no trouble at all in negotiating this descent, and must be marveling at the difficulties being experienced by the white people. For her own part, Cassie was positively enjoying it. She slithered and stumbled along, knowing that it did not matter in the least if she muddied and tore her frock, or displayed too much ankle, or let her hair be caught in overhanging twigs. She felt as light and free as any native bird of this wild undisciplined land, where every privilege must be fought for.

"I—can't—carry—this—cat—much—longer," panted Martha. "He's kicking and spitting all the time."

"I'll take him if you carry the butter-churn," offered Cassie. "I don't think the bottom of the mountain can be much farther now —the track's getting less steep."

Apart from the leveling-out of the path, however, there was nothing to tell them that the actual descent had been accomplished. They plowed on and on through the same dark thick forest, hearing only their own footsteps, for now that they were at sea-level the trees muffled the noise of the surf. Sally-Lou wept with exhaustion, and traveled for a time on Gavin's back; Gavin, with Francis gone, was Missabella's right-hand man, and he seemed actually to have grown in stature, so proud was he of his new position. His Uncle Angus, who back in Switherby had been disturbed by Gavin's poor state of health, would have hardly recognized this sturdy upright youth who walked for miles without complaint—indeed, it was the more muscular and active Luke who grumbled at the hardships of the journey.

Robin, not understanding fully where they were going or why, accepted the situation with an un-childlike patience, occasionally glancing about in wonderment at the unfamiliar and forbidding landscape. Once he dropped back out of sight for a few minutes, and Cassie, sent to retrieve him, found him sitting on a fallen log, staring into the scrub.

"The black boy was here," he told her, not afraid, only a little puzzled.

"I know," said Cassie. "But don't tell the others, Robin. Not yet, anyway. They mightn't like the black boy at first."

Robin nodded by way of agreement, and came willingly enough when she held out her hand to lead him along the track. She told him stories to help pass the time, and Paul and the twins came close to listen also, for Cassie's stories, begun during the voyage out, had become something of a treat to them.

"You sound like a real book," said Marianne admiringly. "Wherever do you get such notions from?"

"Everywhere," said Cassie vaguely. She had a feeling that Eben might be listening too, for his pace—and Jessie's—had slowed perceptibly. To have any other adult in her audience would have embarrassed her, but she did not think of Eben as an ordinary sort of grown-up person. It would have shocked poor Missabella had she known that Cassie looked upon the convict almost as one of the orphans. To Cassie it was perfectly logical, for was not Eben, like themselves, a waif without known relatives and an exile from his own country?

Luke lifted his drooping head suddenly, and sniffed the air.

"I can smell salt," he declared. "And listen—can't you hear the waves?"

Forgetting their weariness, all the children except Gavin ran ahead, breaking through a thicket of some thorny unknown bush to emerge gleefully on a broad sloping shore. Everyone scampered and shouted, their voices startling a flock of gulls which had been nesting below a sand-hill. Cassie ran to the edge of the water, and snatched off her shoes and stockings to wade ankle-deep, rejoicing in the cool clinging feel of wet sand.

Even Phelan could see that a brief rest here was imperative. The horses were so exhausted that they could scarcely stumble across the beach; he lightened their loads and led them a little way into the sea, which was calm and somnolent beneath the warm afternoon sun.

"How much farther now?" asked Missabella, sitting on a dune and fanning herself with her rather bedraggled hat.

"About ten miles. It's fairly easy goin' along the beach, but if the tide's too 'igh we mightn't be able to get across the lake entrance, farther down." Phelan turned and studied the western sky, then spent a few minutes silently contemplating the sea.

"Could be all right," he said at last. "Tide looks to be just on the turn—won't be 'igh for another two or three 'ours. We can't waste much time, though."

Missabella felt his accusing gaze upon her, and rose with a sigh.

"I expect you're right. I shall gather up the children at once. They won't mind so much as long as we are traveling along the beach."

So she rounded up her scattered flock, scolded Cassie for removing her shoes—not merely because it was unladylike, but because of the delay involved in putting them on—and took Sally-Lou's small sandy hand firmly in her own. Slowly and wearily they all marched on again towards the south.

 8

The Clearing on the Hill-top

THEIR FIRST NIGHT in the Illawarra was spent in a cave. To begin with, the children were greatly delighted, for it was quite a splendid cave, tall enough for even the adults to stand up in, and facing across a little bay well protected by reefs, so that the water was perpetually placid. It proved to be an excellent spot for fishing, too, and when they could fish from their own doorstep, as it were, everyone was anxious to try.

"Fish have to be cleaned, you know," Missabella reminded them. "And some of you must gather driftwood for the fire. I think we shall leave the fishing to Gavin and Luke and the two men."

The cave faced south-west, and at this point their own holding was actually in sight, part of an extent of hilly bushland about half a mile inland.

"No use goin' any farther this evenin'," Phelan had said, when he had discovered the cave. "It's too late to start peggin' and fencin', and that there cow is about ready to give up the ghost. She 'as to 'ave a rest."

Missabella felt rather grateful to Jessie for causing such a respite, for Missabella herself was certain that she could

101

not go one step more before morning, and all the children were hungry and sleepy after the long, long day in the open air. So it was with great relief that they unloaded the horses and set about their various tasks. Eben found a sheltered grassy place for Jessie, and built his own fire there; although she was tethered to a tree, he intended to spend the night close beside her, in case any inquisitive native should take a fancy to such a fine animal.

"What about Tomkins?" demanded Paul. "Who's going to look after *him*?"

"Phelan will take good care of the horses, never fear," Missabella reassured him. "But I believe we shall have more trouble with the cat than with all the other animals put together."

***

Certainly Rosie was not in the least imbued with a pioneering spirit. Released from his sack at the back of the cave, he cowered under a shelf of rock and spat and rumbled at all comers. Finally he made a frantic dash for the entrance, and clawed wildly at Gavin, who recovered him just in time.

"Give him some fish," suggested Missabella, and forthwith Marianne and Martha sat patiently on their blankets feeding Rosie with titbits left over from supper, until the cat deigned to settle down between them, leaving them with less than their fair share of blanket.

"This rock is hard," complained Selina. "And I keep hearing queer noises at the back of the cave. Do you suppose it goes much farther in?"

"Doesn't matter if it does," declared Cassie. "There's no

one here but ourselves. It's the sea that makes the noise."

All the same, Cassie for once was grateful for Selina's company. The fire at the mouth of the cave threw strange flickering shadows over the rocky vault that was the roof; the sea growled and muttered in its invisible haunts, so close to the travelers that it was almost as if they were afloat once more, but without a stout hull to protect them and a skilled captain to guide them. For the first time in many months, Cassie remembered clearly what it had been like to have a fixed home, however humble, and a mother to stand between her children and the rigors of the world. How distant and dream-like it seemed now!

"But I don't want to be back in Switherby," Cassie told herself resolutely. "I'm just lonely because Francis isn't here. Tomorrow we shall start making our own new home, and one day Francis will live in it, too."

She sank at last into an uneasy sleep. The fire dwindled to a crimson circle of embers, and beside it Phelan dozed in the manner of any bushman, with some part of his mind conscious enough to be aware at once of any approaching danger, human or of the elements. Missabella slept little; she was alert to every change in the breathing or posture of her charges, wondering whether they were warm and comfortable, whether their supper had been adequate, whether the smaller children would suffer from exhaustion after the trying journey. And, for the hundredth time, she asked herself if she were doing right, leading them into this wilderness which was so much vaster and more formidable than she had ever surmised. But the only voice to answer was the indifferent one of the sea.

Outside, in the grassy patch near the beach, Jessie slept more soundly than anyone, while her guardian, Eben, lay on his back and stared at a few unknown stars sliding now and then from drifts of cloud. Once a light soft rain fell, but Eben merely drew his blanket up to his chin and endured it patiently. The heaviest shower could hardly have alarmed him, when he had suffered in the past year or two every kind of hardship, both physical and otherwise. Like Cassie, he thought of an unpretentious but well-loved home, and of a mother he would not see again. Unlike Cassie, he had no hopes of the future; in actual fact, he was unchained, but was not this country one huge prison, without the faintest possibility of escape? And even if he did escape, to whom and to what would he return?

Only a few yards away, but so well concealed that Eben could have not the faintest suspicion of his presence, Cammy lay curled in the shelter of a rock. He had dug a hole for his bed, and lined it with dry leaves and ferns, and he was tolerably warm and comfortable. He slept soundly, without dreaming, and had he been awake and let his thoughts wander, they would have traveled no farther than the coming day. Cammy lived an hour or so at a time; the planning involved in tracking the white people to the Illawarra had been a great mental effort on his part, and he was glad it was over. What came next was no more to be pondered on than tomorrow's weather.

***

"Somehow I always thought of acres as being flat," remarked Cassie. "However shall we turn all this into a farm?"

Behind her the other children clustered in a damp and shivering group. The rain that had come with the misty dawn had ceased for the moment, but the wind sweeping in from the south was chilly indeed. Even the long climb from the shore to the crest of the hill had failed to warm tired young bodies still aching from yesterday's arduous journey. They were hardly cheered by this first view of their new home; in fact, Sally-Lou looked about her once and burst into tears.

"There isn't even a cave here," she wailed. "Where will we sleep?"

"We're going to build a house," Gavin assured her. "You'll see."

But even Gavin was secretly dismayed. The task of providing any sort of habitation here seemed so enormously difficult that he could scarcely think where to begin. On the eastern side, the slope was fairly gentle, but thickly clothed with every variety of tree and shrub that thrived in this lush region; to north and south, the land dropped away more precipitously, in a series of miniature cliffs and ledges, upon which the undergrowth still managed to survive, though growing at crazy angles. It was impossible to see as yet what lay to the westward, for on the top of the hill the palms and gums were so tall and densely joined that hardly a patch of grey sky showed between them. On the whole property, as far as anyone could judge, there was no clear area greater than five or six feet in diameter.

Missabella gazed at the anxious and miserable faces of the orphans, and fought back her own bitter disappointment. If she once despaired, she told herself, they were all lost, and the long hard pilgrimage from Switherby had been in vain.

"In a few minutes, after I've spoken with Phelan, I shall have work for all of you," she announced, in a fair imitation of her best schoolroom manner. "Meanwhile, you older ones can look for firewood."

If only the rain holds off for a few hours, she implored silently, *and if only Phelan and Eben and the two bigger boys can work hard enough*—but she must stop speculating and do what she could.

Phelan's phlegmatic and unperturbed acceptance of the nature of her holding was a considerable help in itself.

"Country 'ereabouts is all the same," he remarked, leading Tomkins to the shelter of a huge blackbutted gum. "All up an' down an' the divil to clear, but the soil's good, an' there's fresh water not far from 'ere, I'll be bound. Send one or two of the young 'uns to find a spring—them as is old enough to tell fresh water from salt, an' not get lost doin' it."

For this important task Missabella chose Cassie and Luke, as Gavin was obviously going to be needed for more strenuous work. Sure enough, in no time Phelan had unloaded the hatchets, and issued them to Eben and Gavin with instructions to start on the nearest cabbage-palms.

"I'll give 'em a 'and when I've seen to the 'orses," he added. "We can use most every bit of them palms, one way or 'nother."

The children studied the strange bare-trunked trees, rearing straight up to burst suddenly into a wide circle of fronds with a cabbage-like center, and wondered what use such vegetation could possibly be, either erect or fallen. But now no one had much time for idle musings, as Phelan mustered all available hands to assist with the unloading of the baggage. Cassie and Luke took a bucket each, and set out to find water.

"Phelan thinks the western side is the most likely place," Missabella said, waving in that direction. "But don't go out of sight of this hill, and if you think you're lost, call as loudly as you can."

"Of course we won't get lost," Luke remarked confidently, as they began their search. "We know the camp is between us and the sea."

"What if we can't see the ocean, then?" demanded Cassie, who was already acquiring a degree of caution, at least in regard to the dangers of this completely alien country. "Because we won't, in a few minutes."

She was quite right. In no time the barrier of trees had shut out all sight and sound of the grey and white waves, and even the ring of axes on timber seemed to come from a remarkable distance. With not the faintest trace of a path to guide their steps, the children proceeded very gradually downward, stopping frequently to listen for the noise of running water, or to examine the dark soil for any signs of moisture.

"We could spend all day doing this, and still find nothing," Luke said at last, quickly tiring of any undertaking which did not bring immediate results. "I think we ought to go back."

"Fine sort of settler *you'd* be," said Cassie scornfully. "We have to find water, if we want to live here at all."

"I don't know if I do want to," muttered Luke.

A flock of brilliant birds whirred suddenly from near-by tree-tops, and a wallaby hopped briskly away across a flat-topped rock on the children's right. Something flashed through the air in pursuit of the animal, but missed and stuck in the undergrowth. In quick triumphant recognition, Cassie plunged after it, and returned waving a spear at the puzzled Luke.

"I knew Cammy wouldn't be far away! He's just the person to find our water."

She held the spear and waited, enjoining Luke to silence. Presently a wary black face peered over the top of a clump of spiky grass, and Cammy made urgent signs to request the restoration of his weapon.

"You find water, I give you spear," said Cassie firmly, holding up her bucket.

"However did you make friends with the black people so quickly?" asked Luke. "Or—wait a minute—isn't that the boy who followed us from Farm Cove? But how did he get here?"

"Never mind that now," said Cassie impatiently. "He's here, and that's what counts. See—he understands about the water. All we have to do is follow him."

Luke did not share Cassie's complete trust in her new-found friend, but none the less Cammy's beckoning and pointing seemed full of purpose, so Luke followed where he led. It was not easy to keep him always in view, so agile and quick was the small black body, twisting in and out through undergrowth which the white children would have considered impenetrable. Both Cassie and Luke were breathless, scratched, and somewhat torn of clothing when they finally emerged behind Cammy on a little grassy plateau. Below them, and to their left, the ground was flat but swampy, the haunt of wild duck in considerable numbers— Cammy indicated them with a broad smile and an exaggerated pantomime of gastronomic enjoyment, so that Cassie made a mental note to tell Gavin and Missabella where at least one form of food was to be found.

"He doesn't mean we're to fetch water from down there, does he?" asked Luke, peering doubtfully at the greenish pools visible among the reeds.

Cassie and Cammy held another of their peculiar caricatured conversations, from which Cassie concluded:

"No, that swamp is salt. But Cammy thinks there's fresh water down here . . ."

And she pointed to the right, where the hill-side ended in a sort of miniature rocky peninsula, with the swamp on one side and the endless bushy ridges on the other.

"Anyway, there's one good thing," remarked Luke, as he scrambled over the shale, "if the water's so far away, we shan't have to wash very often."

"How shall we ever get the horses and the cow down to drink?" Cassie wondered, looking back up the rugged slope. "Oh, well, I suppose Eben will think of something. He won't let Jessie go thirsty, even if he has to carry the water to her in a bucket."

A shrill cry of what seemed to be triumph from their guide brought them tumbling down into a tiny gully, a shadowy, hidden, remote little place shut off from sky and sun, but holding in its depths a deep still pool. This was fed by a steady flow of water from the precipitous hill on the northwest side; Cassie, cautiously tasting, pronounced the liquid quite fresh and sweet. Cammy agreed with her, and his delight in his own cleverness at finding the precious pool was very evident. Laughing, Cassie handed back his spear, and she and Luke filled their buckets.

"Now all we have to do is make our way back," said Luke. "Shouldn't we mark the trees as we go, so we'll know the track next time?"

"Good idea," said Cassie approvingly. "You're quite good as an explorer, after all. Cammy shall help us."

"Are you going to let Missabella see him, then?"

"Why not? We can tell her how he helped us find the water, and she *must* know how useful he could be out here in the bush. We shan't have to feed him, because he can catch his own food."

Having arranged matters thus to her own satisfaction, if not perhaps to Missabella's, Cassie persuaded Cammy to return with them to the camp. Again he proved his worth as a member of the expedition by discovering the shortest route to the hill-top, and by showing the others how to scratch marks on the bark of trees with a sharp stone. They were relieved to find that even with two heavy buckets to be carried, the return journey was speedier and far less arduous than they had supposed.

The camp on the ridge was by this time such a scene of activity that at first Cammy's presence went unnoticed. Eben and Gavin were still felling the cabbage-palms, while Phelan roped them to control the direction of their fall, and then set to work to strip the leaves and the bark. The twins, Selina, and Paul were all endeavoring, with a weird assortment of tools, to flatten the tough undergrowth and remove the smaller rocks and stones. Missabella, aided by Robin and Sally-Lou, was sorting the stores and bedding, and stowing them under canvas as a precaution against sudden rain.

Cassie marched with her bucket into the center of the tiny clearing, a damp, disheveled, wild-haired figure, but glowing with success and a feeling of accomplishment.

"We found it," she pronounced. "Lots of it, only the track's rather steep. We would never have seen the pool if Cammy hadn't helped us."

Missabella glanced up then, and saw the native boy on the outskirts of the camp, poised ready for flight. Phelan saw only the spear he held, and automatically reached for the gun left loaded and propped against a near-by rock.

"You don't need that!" cried Cassie. "Cammy's our

friend—he followed us all the way from Sydney. He hasn't anyone of his own."

"Now I come to see 'im proper, 'e's only a little feller at that," said Phelan. "S'pose 'e ain't likely to do no 'arm."

And Phelan laid aside the musket and went on with his work. Missabella did not take the affair so calmly, however.

"Do you mean to say, Cassie, that you knew this creature was following us, and told me nothing? How did he know where we were going?"

"He found out while we were still in Chapel Row," said Cassie, rapidly turning sulky as she usually did when reprimanded. "I didn't tell him. I didn't even see him until after we left Mr. Rose's farm. I couldn't have stopped him coming, anyway."

Missabella checked herself as she was about to deliver a brief pointed lecture on the evils of deceit. However wayward Cassie might be, her moral welfare must wait until her physical well-being—and that of her companions—was attended to.

"Thank you for fetching the water, Cassie. You may help the others with the clearing now. Please see that the native boy does not touch any of our belongings."

But Cammy showed no signs of meddling in any way whatsoever. Plainly the activities of the white people were a source of great interest to him; he squatted under a tree and stared solemnly from one to another of the laborers, paying particular wide-eyed attention to Missabella, who still wore her traveling-hat with its sadly tattered green feather. When Robin was released from the work-force, being willing enough but deficient in stamina, Cammy's face brightened, and his nods and smiles brought Robin to share his vantage-point. The pair sat in a silence that was none the less full of fellowship, and when Phelan called a halt for the midday meal, Robin insisted on offering half his portion to his new friend. Although it consisted of Mrs. Rose's best salted beef and bread from her own fine flour, Cammy apparently did not find it to his taste, for he shook his head and presently disappeared into the bush with his spear.

" 'E ain't used to white folks' food yet," observed Phelan. "Fancies a bite o' roast *goanna*, more like."

"If the blacks around here are troublesome, I suppose we might use this boy as a kind of go-between," suggested Missabella, who was beginning to see the practical value of Cammy's presence.

"Mebbe," said Phelan, rather doubtfully. "Probably they belong to a different tribe in these parts, an' they mightn't care for the boy's looks. But 'e'll be a 'elp in other ways, fishin' an' 'untin', an' knowin' 'is way around the bush."

And he surveyed the company at large with a gloomy air, as if to indicate that he thought very little of their collective ability to survive here unaided. Perhaps he decided then and there not to depart for Mount Gilead until the next day, because he continued to work furiously throughout the afternoon. A few light showers fell, but Phelan regarded them as a help rather than a hindrance, for they softened the ground, and made his task of embedding the poles a little easier.

Robin, Paul and Sally-Lou had all retired for an after-dinner nap under the canvas, with a miserable and suspicious Rosie for company. The older children looked on in fascination, occasionally being called on for assistance, as Eben and Phelan created the skeleton of a hut from rough-hewn logs and branches. Not far away, Gavin was putting the finishing-touches to a pen for the animals, a stout if rather unsymmetrical arrangement of crotched poles and cross-pieces, lashed here and there with rope.

"Real 'andy with 'is fingers, that lad is," said Phelan approvingly. "Couldn't 'ardly do better meself."

Gavin, overhearing, turned red with gratification, and was allowed to introduce Jessie and Tomkins to their new home. They had cropped what grass they could from the heavily-timbered hill-top, but as Phelan pointed out, to obtain adequate grazing in the future they must be led down to the relatively clear lands near the beach.

"Them girls can do that, easy," Phelan said. "All they need do is stop the animals strayin', an' keep an eye out for blackfellers."

Selina shuddered at this, but Cassie was delighted at the prospect of such freedom, seeing herself riding Tomkins bareback along the shore, whose bays and headlands she was longing to investigate.

"There won't be much housekeeping in this sort of house, will there?" remarked Martha, regarding the trodden grass and earth that was the floor of their hut. "And we can throw away our mattresses when we get up in the morning."

For the time being they were to sleep on piles of fern laid over strips of canvas, as they had no materials available to fill the striped ticking covers Missabella had brought. Mr. Rose had promised to send down a load of straw later on, but in the meantime the gathering of fern and dry branches would be one more task to add to the growing daily list.

"I think it's going to be the finest little house ever," declared Marianne, watching in admiration as the workers wove palm-leaves into the roof-pieces. "But will that stuff really keep out the rain?"

"We shall soon find out," said Selina, looking up

apprehensively at the heavy grey sky, which was bringing an early twilight. "I hope they can finish the walls in time."

Evidently Phelan had misgivings, too, for he soon set all idle hands to work again, some to gather more wood and feed the fire, others to help split the bark for the sides of the hut. All the water-buckets were set in the open, for the rain must not be wasted, and meanwhile all the food, and valuable items such as the gun and the tools, were stored in a corner of the almost-completed hut.

"Won't be near big enough for all of 'em," Phelan told Missabella, as he stepped back to examine his handiwork. "The boys'll 'ave to build another by 'n by. But meantime, this'll do. I'll camp under the trees with yon convict feller."

Indeed, when all the children—and Rosie—had gathered in the hut, it was sadly overcrowded, but none of the humans really minded. As they ate the evening meal by the uncertain shifting light of tallow candles, the rain began to fall in earnest, pattering and sliding and chuckling on the palm-leaf roof, but Phelan had done his work well, and the few leaks were cheerfully ignored.

"It feels so cosy, like a real home," said Selina wonderingly, for she had expected only damp and discomfort, at the very least.

Missabella glanced around the circle of young faces, and gave one long though inaudible sigh of relief. Everyone was well and unscathed, they had a roof over their heads, livestock in the pen, and enough food to last several weeks. At long last the journey was over, and while the hardships and struggles were only just beginning, Missabella could nevertheless feel reasonably satisfied, even a little proud of her own part on the pilgrimage. It could turn out to be a success, after all.

9

Adventure with a Jersey Calf

"DEAR FRANCIS," Cassie wrote one day in May, "I cannot tell when this letter will reach you, as our only way of sending mail is by sailing-vessel from the Five Islands, or overland by Campbell-town. However, Eben and Gavin are going to the Five Islands tomorrow, in the hope of getting news of a timber-cutter's boat. I wish I could go too, but Missabella says it is not fitting, so I must stay and mind the cow as usual. Jessie had her calf two days after we arrived here, a dear little bull-calf, no use for milk, of course, only for breeding, but that is important. Eben believes we could make our living by breeding dairy cattle, as the Illawarra is suited to it. We named the calf Michael, after Mr. Phelan who was so good to us and built our hut. He was a grumpy old creature, but very, very helpful.

"In our first week it rained most of the time, and we had to put more palm-leaves on the roof. After Mr. Phelan had left we were all rather dismal, being so alone, but Missabella made us work so hard we forgot to grumble. Gavin has been by far the busiest, and we could never do without him, only he is quiet and serious all the time, like an old man. Luke prefers to shirk the hardest jobs, like digging the ground for planting, and wants to be off shooting or fishing. I must say he is rather good at finding food for us, with the help of Cammy, the black boy who followed us from Sydney. Cammy has made his own funny little shelter down the hill from us, and catches his own meals, but he is a good friend to have, and looks after Robin, the one Cammy seems to like best. Perhaps it is because Robin is lame and not at all clever, and Cammy can understand that.

"Martha and Marianne have become the dairy-maids, milking Jessie and setting the milk and making butter. They made milk-pails out of the bark of the tree called the cabbage-palm, and out of the leaves they are making big spreading hats for the boys. We have all helped with the planting of potatoes and maize, but it may be too late in the year for them. One of Paul's jobs is to keep the birds away from the cultivated patch. Sometimes I think he is making friends with the parrots instead of frightening them. Even Sally-Lou has her work to do, for she must sweep out the hut each morning, and gather firewood. As you will guess, Selina is the one who looks after our clothes, washing them as well as mending. She seems a great deal happier now.

"I *never* wish I were back in Switherby, we are so busy and lively here. It is like a little world on its own. Missabella wants to call our place Mount St. Matthew, after the vicarage, but it does seem a grand sort of name for two huts and a cattle-pen in the middle of the bush . . ."

After this prolonged bout of writing, Cassie suddenly stopped and chewed her pencil. There was something else she wanted to write, but she was not sure how to express it, even in her own mind. She sat up and contemplated the scene before her, hugging her thin bony knees that jutted through her well-worn and outgrown skirt. She had shed her shoes and stockings, as she always did once she was out of sight of Missabella.

It was a brilliant morning, bright as a jewel and soft as silk. The little round-browed headland where Cassie sat was brushed gently by long idle waves; on either side of her the sea was so blue and limitless that it made her eyes ache to watch it. And although May in the Colony was the last month of autumn, the sun had a solid comforting warmth, and the trees clustering thickly along the shore had shed neither color nor foliage. Cassie had soon come to know every detail of this sheltered little bay, only half a mile from home, yet as remote and untouched as a desert island. Down to her left a creek ran out across the beach, the same creek that fed the swamp behind the camp; it was too slight a waterway to have any official name, so the children had called it Switherby Brook.

Cassie loved this place, and the free adventurous life that she lived here. The word "unladylike" had not been spoken for weeks; she need no longer suffer through lessons on deportment and embroidery and etiquette. No one had time now to wonder whether Cassie would ever be as refined and comely as a growing girl ought to be; she had turned twelve last week, and though the occasion had been duly marked by a special high tea, with cold roast duck and the first serving of the twins' own brand of cheese, Missabella had refrained from making her usual observation that Cassie must try and behave more like a young gentlewoman and less like a boy. After all, it was Cassie's very boyishness, her energy and determination, that had been one of Missabella's chief supports.

No, thought Cassie, I cannot complain any longer that I am not allowed to be myself. The trouble is, I don't seem to know any more just what I *am*. When I worked at my lessons in Switherby, I at least knew that I was clever at book-learning. Here there are no books and no lessons, and although I'm so happy, it's rather as if I were drifting nowhere in particular. If only there were someone to talk to about the future, someone like Francis . . .

She had been staring over the bay without seeing anything clearly, so absorbing were her thoughts. Now she roused herself, for it must be nearly dinner-time, and Jessie and Michael must be returned to their pen. In fact, she could hear Jessie mooing, as if to remind her herdswoman of her duties. Hastily Cassie collected her papers, and ran down to the beach.

"All right, Jessie, I'm coming," she told the unseen animal. "There's no need to fuss."

There was indeed a sort of desperate note to Jessie's lowing, and Cassie realized guiltily that she had seen neither cow nor calf for quite half an hour. She plunged into the scrub on the southern bank of Switherby Brook, and almost cannoned into the ample shape of Jessie, who was pointing her velvet nose towards the creek and looking as agitated as is possible for a stout Jersey cow of meek disposition.

"What's the matter?" demanded Cassie, for like Eben and most of the other children, she was given to talking freely to the animals. "Where's Mike?"

Reaching the bank, which was sandy and soft, she peered towards the dappled amber water and at once had her question answered. Mike had somehow found his way on to a spur of sand which was rapidly diminishing under the combined onslaught of his weight and the fast flow of the creek; he was beginning to struggle and flounder, without gaining any ground.

"Hold on, I'll help you," said Cassie confidently, and then belatedly paused to consider just how her help was to be given. Mike was only a few weeks old, but already he was of substantial and stocky build, and Cassie was not at all sure that her own strength was equal to the task of pushing or pulling him to shore.

Behind her, Jessie gave another anguished bellow, and suddenly Cassie stood rigid with horror as the full implications of Mike's plight became clear. It was not simply that Mike might topple off his sand-spit a few yards from the bank; with Cassie's assistance, he would probably escape unscathed. The far greater danger lay in the fact that the tide was running out, and the creek water flowing faster and faster towards the ocean. Any minute Mike would be swept downstream to the shore, and the channel where creek met sea was quite deep enough to allow the passage of even a tubby bull-calf. Once beyond the channel, and in the bay, Mike would be as good as lost.

Cassie drew a deep breath and tried not to panic. It was absolutely unthinkable that Mike should be drowned through her own carelessness. In the space of a few minutes—precious minutes, as the treacherous water lapped at the calf's legs now—she sought to envisage the exact whereabouts of each member of Missabella's household. The girls would be in or about the huts, preparing the dinner, and in any case they would be of little use. Missabella herself would be supervising them, while Paul and Robin dug in the potato patch. Gavin and Luke, she remembered, had gone hunting, and no doubt Cammy was with them. That left only Eben—

"Of course!" cried Cassie. "He was going out to cut palms.

He'll have a rope."

She knew from her constant explorations that an exceptionally fine grove of cabbage-palms flourished half-way up the hill-side,and thither she ran, throwing a word of encouragement to Jessie as she went. Cassie was agile and fleet of foot, but this was no country for sprinting; the paths from Mount St. Matthew to the bay had not yet been trodden often enough to be clearly defined, and Cassie's progress was a series of frenzied dodges as she swerved to avoid rocks and prickly bushes and tree-ferns. She was sobbing with exhaustion as she scrambled upwards; her shoes had been left on the headland, and her feet were bleeding from a dozen scratches.

But she found Eben. No sight in all the world could have been more welcome to Cassie then than the slight, stooped figure of the convict, busily stripping the leaves of the palms and tying them in bundles. Best of all, his strong coil of rope lay beside him, and Cassie snatched it up, panting as she did so:

"Come quick, Eben! Mike's going to drown!"

Eben never wasted words, and after one startled glance at Cassie's face, he followed her down the hill at her own headlong pace. There was plenty of noise to guide them, for to Jessie's lamentations had been added the frantic youthful lowing of her son, now struggling out of his depth, and every moment drifting farther eastwards. Only fifty yards separated him from the channel; soon he would leave the shelter of the trees and be swept past the beach.

"Can you swim?" demanded Eben of his companion, but Cassie shook her head miserably.

Then all at once the convict was completely in charge of the situation.

"I'll go in farther down, with the rope," he said, kicking off his shoes. "You must follow me along the bank, and catch one end of the rope when I throw it. Don't miss."

Cassie nodded, and saw him run and dive well ahead of the calf, with the rope secured round his waist. He had little enough time to undo it, for the gap between him and the animal closed with terrifying speed. Cassie, keeping level with him on the sand, was certain that Mike would be carried right on past his rescuer, but Eben was wonderfully quick, and after a few anguished moments during which man and calf threshed wildly together in the water, Cassie saw his arm come up with the free end of the rope.

"Now!" he yelled. "And hang on for all you're worth!"

The rope landed just short of Cassie's feet, and she slid forward and lay full length on the sand, grasping the end just as it snaked back towards the water. A tremendous pull seemed about to jerk her arms from their sockets, as she fought both the weight of the calf and the powerful drag of the tide; she was slithering over the sand when Eben scrambled out and came to her aid.

"There's a tree back there I can tie the rope to," gasped Eben. "Just a few more pulls and we'll do it."

It was a dismal, bedraggled, bemused lump of Jersey calf that finally struggled on to the beach and collapsed in a grunting heap. But he was alive, quite definitely so, as he showed by attempting to rise when his frantic mother came lumbering to greet him with affectionate nudges.

"We'll just let him warm up in the sun for a bit," said Eben. "Then we must get him back to the pen and give him a rub-down."

Cassie knew that she had no hope of keeping the morning's events a secret. Even if she could explain away

Mike's damp condition, what of Eben, who was not only soaked, but fully clothed? And what of her own appearance? She was covered in wet sand, right to her hair; her feet were torn and stained, and her dress, an ancient garment to start with, was now something which even a beggar might spurn.

"I suppose I shall have to tell Missabella what happened," she said gloomily. "Anyway, it's only fair that everyone should know you rescued Mike."

Eben stood coiling his rope, and said nothing. The crisis over, he was once more the silent and submissive creature whose presence the others all took completely for granted. But for the first time Cassie saw him as a real person, noticing that his features were fine and regular, his blue eyes wide and thoughtful under roughly trimmed fair hair. He had filled out a little since coming to the Illawarra, despite his hard work, and he looked years younger than he had on the day when Missabella fetched him from the barracks. Yet his shoulders still had the old hopeless droop.

"When did you learn to swim?" Cassie asked curiously.

"We swam in the mill-pond when I was a lad," answered Eben. "We just taught ourselves."

He spoke well, Cassie reflected, for a disgraced apprentice.

"You could easily have been carried right out," observed Cassie, gazing at the shining but menacing sea beyond the channel. "I think you were very brave."

"Wouldn't make much difference if I did drown," muttered Eben, so low that Cassie barely heard him. Hear him she did, however, and she was deeply shocked.

"You mustn't say that. Missabella could never manage here without you—I've heard her tell Gavin. Don't you like it here, then?"

"I like working with the animals, and being outdoors so much," said Eben, in a slow way that suggested he was putting his feelings into words for the first time in many years. "It's a pretty spot, and everyone's kind. I'm lucky, compared to some. But it's having no choice that's the trouble. I'm never free, you see."

Cassie nodded, for resenting restraint herself, she could understand the bitterness of continual lack of freedom. After all, Eben was only ten years older than she was, and should have had the best part of his life ahead of him.

"We ought to be going," said Eben. "Mike's on his feet now."

Cassie directed the calf towards the homeward path, which he took willingly enough. Eben followed with Jessie.

"I shall have to come back for my shoes," said Cassie, treading with painful care. "And I expect the letter I was writing to my brother will be rather wet and sandy in my pocket. I was thinking about him, you see, when I let Mike and Jessie wander."

"I should like to be able to write," said Eben unexpectedly. "I can read a little, being in the printing trade, and our mother taught us to speak decent. But she had no time to teach us letters."

"I could write her a letter if you want me to," said Cassie.

"She's dead," said the voice behind her, flatly.

They toiled upwards in silence for the next five minutes, then Cassie went on:

"If you really want to learn to read and write, I can teach you. I used to help Missabella teach the younger children when we were in Switherby."

"You're very kind, Miss," said the expressionless voice,

and Cassie sensed that Eben was raising his defensive bar-
riers again as they drew near to home.

"My name's Cassie," she said over her shoulder.

Now it was Eben's turn to be shocked.

"Miss Braithwaite would never allow that, Miss."

Cassie paused to regain her breath. Above them on the
ridge she could see the beginnings of the cleared land, and
the blue smoke of the cooking-fire rising straight and slow
over the tree-tops.

"All right," said Cassie. "I don't want to get you into
trouble. But I meant what I said about the reading and writing. I don't believe Missabella could object to that. After
all, I might have to go and be a governess one day, to earn
my living, and I need practice."

If Eben saw anything ludicrous in the idea of his shaggy-
haired, graceless companion taking up the genteel post of
governess, then of course he kept it to himself. He was used
to having no human confidant, and he had learned to adopt
the attitudes of recluse as being the only ones available to
him. But to his own surprise, he had actually enjoyed the
brief sociability of the morning.

As Cassie had anticipated, their entry into the camp was
made to the accompaniment of excited questions and exclamations. But Cassie gave the full story to no one but
Missabella, while Eben led Jessie and Mike back to their
pen.

Missabella was watching her two red-faced and anxious
cooks, Martha and Marianne, while they bent over the fire
tending a huge pan of frying fish. The daily menu was a
constant problem to Missabella; until they could procure
more supplies of salted pork and beef, they must rely on the
hunters and fishermen, with the occasional addition of

ducks' eggs, and the children's appetites were so hearty that it took a great deal to satisfy them. For breakfast they ate porridge made from the dwindling store of oatmeal, followed by the flat but substantial bread, which was little more than dough cooked in the ashes of the fire. Their only vegetable at present was the "cabbage" from the palm-trees; nobody liked it much, but under Missabella's stern and vigilant gaze it had to be eaten. Fortunately there was a relative abundance of milk, and each child had a ration of butter and cheese. Jessie's production must inevitably dwindle, however, and Missabella, after much calculation, had decided that the purchase of a second cow should come before that of a plow. And then she must plant some fruit-trees, apple and orange, and seek some advice on the growing of suitable vegetables, other than potatoes . . .

With so many urgent problems to consider and solve, with nine young creatures dependent on her for very existence, Missabella was understandably horrified when Cassie confessed that she had almost lost one of the party's most valued possessions, and risked the life of their only adult laborer into the bargain.

"I should never have allowed you to guard the cattle on your own," said Missabella on a note of real despair. "But I thought I could trust you, and there was no one else to spare. Tomorrow I shall have to send Luke and Selina, and you must take over all Selina's tasks. We'll be short-handed already, with Gavin and Eben going to the Five Islands."

"I could go instead of Gavin, and he could do the hunting as usual," said Cassie, with a quite unwarranted hope.

"Certainly not. If you want privileges, you must earn them. Now go and change those clothes, and try and find a pair of shoes. You must go out immediately after dinner and fetch your own."

Cassie spent most of the afternoon digging more ground for the kitchen garden. It was the hardest work of all, for the soil was sticky and stubborn, and sported a variety of tough weeds. But Cassie found that after an hour or two she felt oddly soothed and restored. She was prepared now to admit that she had been gravely at fault in neglecting the cattle, and she promised herself that she would make amends. She had no wish to vex or disappoint Missabella, for whom she had a deep respect and affection, and she had another, altogether new reason for wanting to behave in a responsible fashion—she would like to show Eben that she could be entrusted with his friendship.

***

Two days later, in the one tranquil waking hour afforded to the inhabitants of Mount St. Matthew—the interval between milking-time and supper—Cassie and Eben took up the positions that in the weeks to come would be wholly familiar to the others, and gradually accepted. Cassie sat on a tree-stump half-way between the huts and the cattle-pen, while Eben arranged the slab of bark that did duty as a writing-desk, and settled beside her on the grass. Writing-paper was scarce and precious, so the pupil used a slate and crayon belonging to Sally-Lou. With these he carefully copied the letters that Cassie showed him, and repeated them aloud. The concentration of both teacher and student was so intense that progress was quite rapid; in no time, it seemed, Eben had advanced from "ABC" to whole words and then short sentences.

Missabella had had misgivings at first, for it had been

her policy to keep the children away from the convict as much as possible. But in this small and utterly isolated community such segregation proved unworkable. Eben in no way forgot his station, as Missabella might have expressed it, yet somehow the children came to look on him as one of the family, just as they accepted Cammy as a fellow-orphan. Missabella comforted herself with the thought that one day Eben would obtain his ticket-of-leave, and then doubtless Mount St. Matthew would know him no more.

"Why don't you teach Cammy to read and write, too?" asked Paul one evening. "He can speak a little English now."

"I could try," said Cassie doubtfully. "But he might not want to learn. Eben does, you see."

Cammy, when shown the slate and made to understand what was afoot, simply grinned and shook his head, and departed to help Robin look for the mythical platypus that the younger children claimed to have seen once on the bank of the creek. Formal education was evidently not in Cammy's line; in other respects, however, he was an instructor himself, being an invaluable guide to the hunters, and an authority on all the native flora and fauna. To date, no encounter had been made with any of the Illawarra aborigines, although they had been glimpsed occasionally on fishing expeditions. Cammy made no attempt to approach them, being apparently satisfied with the new life he had chosen for himself as a sort of attachment to the white camp.

As Eben's education progressed, Cassie gradually learnt something of his past history—not a great deal, as Eben ventured no information without being asked, and Cassie, inquisitive though she was, tried hard to be tactful.

"We must have lived quite close to each other in England," she said one day. "Have you ever been to Switherby?

It's not very big, but it has steam-factories and a mill. It's near Bingleton."

"I know Bingleton," admitted Eben. "My father's folks came from there. We visited them once when I was a little lad. We rode in the farm-cart, I remember."

"Did you live on a farm, then? Is that why you like cows?"

"We weren't there very long. Father died, and we moved to the city so Mother could go to work. Nothing went right, after that," added Eben, slowly tracing letters on his slate.

"Our father was killed at Waterloo," Cassie could not resist saying.

"There's worse ways of dying," muttered Eben. "Like starving. That's what happened to my mother, when she couldn't go to work any more. They put her in the work-house when I went to prison."

Cassie, feeling herself to be out of her depth in such adult tragedies, said nothing, but sat watching a flock of red and blue rosellas whirling across the evening sky. She was quite surprised when Eben said:

"I stole something to get money for her. I meant to fetch the greatcoat out of pawn before I was found out, but I couldn't do it in time."

He scowled at his slate, and rubbed out a misspelled word.

"You mean, you were transported for ten years for taking someone's coat?" asked Cassie. "Even when you were only trying to help your mother?"

"Nobody ever cares what you did it for," said Eben. "You do a wrong thing once, and you're finished. Some of the lads on the ship coming out were hardly older than you."

"If it hadn't been for Missabella, we could have ended up in prison, too," Cassie reflected. "Or the work-house, which wasn't much better. It makes me want to work really hard here, so we can make the place a proper home, and not have to worry about being poor ever again. Do you think we can?"

Eben gave one of his infrequent smiles.

"Why not? You're all young and strong enough."

"And you? Don't you want to stay, even if you get your pardon?"

Eben glanced about the clearing, which had grown sufficiently in recent weeks to give some appearance of permanence. The vegetable patches were flourishing, and diligently tilled; there were even a few transplanted wildflowers growing beside the doorway of the girls' hut. In the pen under the tallest gums, Jessie, Mike and Tomkins drowsed in friendly tranquillity, undisturbed by the antics of Rosie, who was scampering up and down tree-trunks enjoying his customary before-dark exercise.

"It's a big 'if', but it does begin to seem a little like home," Eben admitted.

10

Two Runaways

CASSIE'S LETTER, AFTER lengthy delays, finally reached Francis in Chapel Row at the end of June. It had rested awhile with other mail in the hut of one of the few settlers at the Five Islands, then been put aboard a timber-carrying vessel which traveled as far south as Shoalhaven Heads before making its laborious return journey to Sydney. Its bearer to its ultimate destination was none other than Susannah's friend, Harry of the black beard.

"We're getting married after his next trip," Susannah told Francis during his dinner-break. "Harry's done well with this cedar-cutting, well enough to build a bit of a house out Liverpool way. So I mightn't be here much longer."

Francis murmured some polite congratulations, but his heart was not in them. He would miss Susannah, who not only saw to his material comforts and darned his stockings, but was also his sole confidant and adviser. Mrs. Peachey was too brisk and busy to provide more than a superficial attention to his wants, and the other boarders were either elderly and aloof, or young and married, and therefore wholly absorbed in their own affairs.

"When is Harry's next trip, then?" asked Francis, to keep the conversation going and thus beguile the time until he must go back for afternoon school.

"Oh, he's off again next week, down south again. It's proper hard work, he says, but the country's rich in timber thereabouts. Is that a letter from your folks?"

"From my sister. She seems quite happy, and everyone's well. They're going to breed dairy cattle," added Francis wistfully, longing to see the new calf for himself.

"Mucky things, cows," said Susannah cheerfully. "But I expect there's money in milk and cheese and that. Your Miss Braithwaite will need money, I'll be bound, to feed and clothe all those young ones."

"I know," said Francis. He rose reluctantly from the now deserted table and went into the hall to put on his cap and jacket. It was a quarter to two, quite time for him to leave. He put Cassie's letter in his pocket.

He walked rapidly to keep out the early-winter cold, not out of eagerness for further study, or a desire to be reunited with his schoolfellows. So far he had made few friends, partly because he was by nature reserved and rather shy, and partly because he had failed to find a common meeting ground. Most of the other boys were sons of the Colony's more elevated citizens, highly-placed government officials, or landowners and gentlemen farmers. Francis found his own status difficult to define; he was not ashamed of his ancestry, certainly, nor of Missabella, sister of a respectable vicar, but he had to admit that as an orphan with a middle-aged spinster for a guardian, and a home that was either a boardinghouse or a hut in the wilderness, he could not compete with the other boys in offering hospitality or bragging of opulent surroundings. And as he did not dare to invite any of them back to Mrs. Peachey's after school or on Saturdays, he was severely handicapped in the forming of friendships, for the boys were a gregarious lot, accustomed to visiting one another's homes.

As for his studies—Francis often regretted now that he had not made his own ambitions plain long ago. Somehow he had been persuaded that he was suited to a life of scholarship and the company of books; he was quickly learning the gravity of this error. He liked to read and pore over maps and diagrams, and he took a certain pride in the neatness of his handwriting and drawings, but in the intricacies of Latin and Greek he was thoroughly lost. He often wished that Cassie could take his place, for how eagerly would she have swallowed such liberal helpings of the classics, as well as history and English grammar and divinity! Her mind was so much more agile and sharp than his, yet who had ever heard of a girl receiving a classical education? Why had a capricious and contrary fate sent Cassie to till the soil and herd cattle, while Francis, who wanted only to be a farmer, was sentenced to years of study he could not appreciate?

One of the boys from his form, a lively athletic fellow called Edgeley, joined Francis at the corner of Hunter Street. Edgeley was easy-going and sociable, and did not mind walking a few yards with this queer young Brown. Behind his back they called him "the Oyster," because he was so close about his affairs.

"Back to the old grind, eh?" said Edgeley affably. "Three jolly old hours with the Doctor, sweating over that beastly Caesar. Who cares about the Gallic Wars, anyway? Latin won't be any use to me when I'm out helping my father on the farm."

"I thought you lived in the town," said Francis, whose acquaintance with Edgeley was fairly slight. He had seen him sometimes after school, leading a group of cronies along Chapel Row.

"I live in town with my mother and brothers, so that we can go to school," Edgeley explained. "But my father spends most of his time on the place out near Windsor, and when I'm old enough I'll join him. One of Father's friends is Mr. Macarthur, and do you know what he says about the good old Grammar School? He told Father it wouldn't last more than a few months, because the Doctor can't see eye to eye with the trustees."

Francis was keenly interested in the latter part of this speech. He knew little enough of John Macarthur—only that he bred sheep, and had a finger in most Colonial pies—but such a confident statement concerning the school's future might be worthy of belief.

"You mean, we shall all have to leave?"

"No, not exactly, because the Doctor could carry on his own school under a different name. It wouldn't be the Sydney Free Grammar School any more. I don't much care—Father is thinking of sending us to the Georgian School next year, the one Mr. Cape has."

Francis wondered whether his benefactor, Mr. Rose, knew of this threatened upheaval, and if so, whether he would remove him from Dr. Halloran's establishment. If fees must be paid in future, then whoever would pay them?

Edgeley, untroubled by any financial worries, skipped to another subject. He loved to talk, and the identity of his listener did not really matter much.

"Out on the Nepean we have four convicts working for us. We did have five, only one got away last week. I said I didn't believe he'd get far—they usually get lost and starve, or the blacks finish them off—but Father told me this Gracechurch was a crafty rascal, and probably had been planning his escape for weeks."

Francis suddenly stood still, a few yards from the school gateway.

"Did you say 'Gracechurch'?"

Edgeley glanced back at him in surprise.

"Yes, I did. The name stuck in my mind, because it was a bit out of the ordinary. What's the matter? You couldn't possibly know the fellow—he was a regular scoundrel, a hulking, surly sort of chap with a sandy beard."

"No, I don't know him," answered Francis truthfully. "I thought I'd heard the name somewhere, that's all."

During the afternoon he found it even more difficult than usual to track down ablatives and gerundives through the dense thickets of Latin prose. The Doctor berated him, and the other boys derived a welcome amusement from Brown's eccentricities of translation. Finally Dr. Halloran ordered Francis to do extra preparation that night, uttering many dire predictions about penalties for incorrect work, and concluding:

"If you don't improve, Brown, I shall be obliged to inform Mr. Rose that you do not deserve your free place in this establishment."

"Yes, sir," muttered Francis.

Dr. Halloran sighed, and released him. The headmaster indeed rather liked this quiet, pleasant-faced boy, who tried hard and gave no trouble as far as his behavior was concerned—it was just a pity that the lad was not suited for classical scholarship, and never would be.

Francis went home alone, his books under one arm, and

his hands thrust deep into his trouser-pockets for warmth. The sun had already disappeared beyond the Rocks, and the little township, huddled around the waterfront, was half lost in misty shadow. Smoke rose from the chimneys of Chapel Row, and the air smelt sharply and pleasantly of numerous dinners a-cooking. Normally Francis would have been comforted by the prospect of Mrs. Peachey's laden table, but this evening he was hardly interested in food. Again and again his thoughts reverted to Edgeley's account of Gracechurch's escape; *could* it be the same man? Had Robin really seen his father at Gravesend? Francis had never set eyes on Gracechurch, but Edgeley's description could be made to fit. The twins had sandy hair, and Martha had said once that her father was a big man, taller than the vicar.

"Well, what if it *is* Gracechurch?" Francis asked himself inwardly. "He can't know the children are in the Colony, and in any case he went away and left them—he probably doesn't want to see them again. And as Edgeley says, the fellow is sure to starve to death in the bush. So why worry?"

Yet somehow Francis was still worrying and wondering that night, long after he should have been asleep. Cassie's letter, Harry's talk of the Illawarra, Edgeley's gossip concerning the Grammar School, and his news of a man called Gracechurch—all these had combined to give Francis an overpowering longing to visit his fellow-orphans, and tell Missabella at first-hand of recent developments. He felt instinctively that she must be warned of the possibility of Gracechurch's presence in the Colony, and a letter would take so long to reach her.

"I suppose Harry would take it, on his next voyage," thought Francis. "If only I could go myself!"

Francis was a responsible and cautious boy, not given to

acting on impulse, so the idea that had just sprung into his head was dismissed at first as absurd. Of course he could not go off on his own to the Illawarra—he must stay at school, and try to master that bothersome Latin. Missabella had insisted on it.

He turned over once again and stared at the moonlit oblong between the shutters. He reminded himself that he was thirteen years old, that at such an advanced age the majority of boys were already earning their own livings, and that he, Francis Brown, was simply wasting his time poring over Caesar's Gallic Wars and Greek philosophy. Dr. Halloran himself obviously realized this plain fact. Somehow, for the good of everyone, Missabella must be made to understand, and there was only one way to go about the task—he must approach her in person, for he could never put his thoughts effectively into writing. If she forced him to return to school, then he must come back and resign himself to his fate. But to begin with, he was going to put up a fight.

Thus sternly resolved, Francis fell into a deep and peaceful sleep. In the morning he rose early enough to finish off his hated Latin, and ate a hearty breakfast.

"You're looking blooming this morning," observed kindhearted Susannah. "That letter from your sister must have cheered you up."

"I suppose it did," agreed Francis. "When did you say Harry's ship was sailing?"

"Next Wednesday, he thinks. But he'll be round for supper tonight—you can ask him yourself, if you're wanting him to carry a letter for you."

Francis lingered after school that evening at the corner of Chapel Row and King Street, for it was up King Street that Harry usually came, from his lodgings near the barracks. Francis recognized him as soon as he turned out of George Street—there was no mistaking the burly, black-bearded figure, though today it was clad in respectable dark worsted jacket and trousers, with light-colored waistcoat and pale-blue cravat. Obviously Harry was in his most jovial mood, for as he came he was singing loudly and gaily of the Bailiff's Daughter of Islington, and a few elegant ladies out for an evening stroll drew quickly away from him, no doubt suspecting that the sawyer had been partaking too freely of the colonial rum.

"Well now, if it ain't young Francis!" exclaimed Harry. "I thought you'd be busy with them books of yours. How's that Caesar chap gettin' on?"

Harry took a keen though puzzled interest in the progress of the Gallic Wars, as related by Francis in Mrs. Peachey's kitchen after supper, but this time he was to be deprived of the latest instalment.

"I wanted to ask you something very important," Francis said anxiously. "And I don't want Mrs. Peachey to hear. I shall tell Susannah all about it if it comes off."

Harry, believing Francis to be planning some sort of escapade at school, sat down on the edge of a drinking-trough and assumed a suitably solemn expression. It became sober in earnest, however, as Francis went on:

"I have some news I want to take to Miss Braithwaite, and I don't want to put it in a letter. May I go to the Illawarra with you next week?"

Harry scratched his head in perplexity, and surveyed the boy before him. In the soft rosy twilight Francis' face looked paler and finer-drawn than any thirteen-year-old visage should be, and his dark eyes held a kind of unyouthful desperation.

"Come," said Harry, with surprising gentleness. "Why do you really want to go? It ain't just because of this news you've got hold of, is it?"

"No," admitted Francis. "I don't think I can stand being here on my own any more. I don't like school, and I shall never be any good at Latin and Greek. I would be much more useful on the farm, I know. I tried to explain to Miss Braithwaite, but she didn't understand. Perhaps she will, now."

"And what if she sends you right back?" demanded Harry.

"That would take a little time. And at least I would have seen them all, and the property, and if I *had* to come back, I should be able to think about all the things they were doing, and it wouldn't seem quite so lonely."

Privately, Harry was already on Francis' side. He had told Susannah weeks ago that it was a shame to let the boy stay cooped up with his books, when all his friends and relations were so far away. After all, the boy was an orphan to start with, so it was downright cruel to leave him with no one but Mrs. Peachey to turn to. That Latin and stuff was all very fine, thought Harry, but since when did it take the place of a family?

"It ain't all that easy," said Harry at last, with some regret. "I just can't ask you to come along as a passenger, and you're too young to sign on for work—you ain't had the experience, neither."

"I could come if I paid my passage, couldn't I?" asked Francis eagerly. "You do take passengers sometimes, don't you?"

"If there's room enough, and I don't suppose you'd take up much," mused Harry. "I could find out how much you'd have to pay. Can't promise we'll be puttin' in at the Five Islands this trip, but we might call at Kiarmi."

Francis was not at all sure where the latter place was in relation to Missabella's holding; however, this seemed a minor detail just then. The big problem was one of finance, and over that Francis pondered at length during the evening. Missabella had left with Mrs. Peachey a small fund to cover his board and a few additional items such as any necessary clothing, but Francis knew he could not recover the money without telling Mrs. Peachey of his planned escape, and he was certain she would do her best to prevent it. He had only a few pence of his own, and no possessions of value apart from his books and the rather battered old watch and chain his father had left him.

"I should hate to sell it," he thought. "Cassie would be furious, because it's all we have to remind us of Father and Mother. And I promised her I would let her have my books when I'd finished with them, so I must try and take them with me."

But one thing was going to be superfluous in the Illawarra, and that was a suit of fine clothes. He still had the old garments he had worn on the voyage from Switherby, and it would not really matter if they were shabby and outgrown—Selina, he remembered, was skilled enough with her needle to alter and repair them.

Francis spent the next few days in an unenviable state of suspense and nervousness. He was not an adventurer at heart, and at times the enormity of his proposed illegal expedition weighed heavily on his conscience. Would Missabella forgive the loss of the clothes she had so carefully chosen for him, or worse still, the waste of the higher education by which she set so much store? He told himself firmly that he would go on working at his books as long as she wished, if only he could stay with her and the other children.

Meanwhile, he had to continue wearing his best suit to school, so as to attract no attention to his plans, and to make all his small preparations in secret. On the evening before Harry's ship was to sail, he confided at last in Susannah.

"I thought something was afoot," said Susannah. "I've been watching you and Harry with your heads together. I only hope you get to this 'ere farm safe and sound, a bit of a lad like you. They say it's as easy as wink to get lost out in the bush."

"Harry drew me a sort of map," explained Francis. "He put in the Five Islands and Kiarmi, and where he thinks Missabella's place might be."

"I wouldn't trust to Harry's drawing," said Susannah gloomily. "He can't hardly write his name, let alone do maps. But there— you might as well be with your sister and brother and friends, instead of moping round here. I shan't say anything to Mrs. Peachey till you've gone, and I'll see you get a fair share of food for the journey."

Thus encouraged, Francis told her of his intention to sell his clothes, and once again she proved a valuable ally.

"Don't just go and try the first clothes-dealer you see," she warned. "He'll cheat you, sure as my name's Susannah Wood. Now I'll tell you what we'll do—"

Her plan was a sound one, as Francis had to admit, but he still felt a little guilty at the deception involved. The next morning he stayed in bed and let Susannah inform Mrs. Peachey that he was not well enough to go to school. Indeed, he did not have to do much pretending—he was too excited and tense to eat his breakfast, and his head ached from concentration on the details of the day's activities. He was to be aboard the timber-cutters' boat, the *Jane Maria,* by noon; its sailing-time was dependent on tides and winds, and therefore indefinite, but Harry thought they would leave early in the afternoon. She was moored at Cockle Bay, and Susannah said that was easy enough to find—you simply kept the Rocks on your right hand and headed west, past the barracks.

While Francis languished in his verandah bed, Susannah slipped out to sell his clothes, stowed away in her market-basket. She was gone so long that Francis feared she had been knocked down by a dray, or set upon by thieves. The faithful old watch showed eleven o'clock when he at last heard her step on the path.

"I did my best for you," Susannah said in a loud whisper, taking out her purse. "I had to go to a number of places before I could get a fair price. But I think this will be enough. I sold the shirts and neckerchief too."

"You didn't take my shoes, did you?" asked Francis anxiously, not relishing a tramp through the Illawarra on bare feet.

"No, though you get a good amount for real leather ones, I'm told," Susannah said rather regretfully—for she dearly loved bargaining in the markets. "Come along, now—you must get dressed, and I'll keep watch. I shall tell Mrs. Peachey you're sleeping."

"I hope you won't get into trouble over this," said Francis. "I've written a letter to Mrs. Peachey, and I've told her it wasn't your fault."

"Never mind that. She won't fuss for long, and anyway I'll be away from here myself soon. Shouldn't be surprised if I didn't see you again some day, if I can make Harry take me on one of his trips."

She bustled off to fetch a parcel of food, and Francis scrambled into his clothes. He put on as many of his old garments as he possibly could squeeze into, for protection against the cold, and to save carrying too much luggage. His books almost filled his kit-bag, and made it quite formidably heavy, but nothing would persuade him to leave them behind.

"You do look different in them old things, and no mistake," observed Susannah. "Anyone would think you were just a street urchin."

With this doubtful tribute sounding in his ears, Francis bade her a grateful farewell and crept out into the back garden. The yard was so small that he had crossed it in a few hurried paces; behind the privet hedge was a gap in the paling-fence, discovered many weeks ago, and this led into the overgrown garden of an empty house in Pitt Street. Through this Francis struggled as fast as his load would permit, nor did he slacken his pace until he had safely crossed George Street.

A brisk dusty wind met him as he climbed to the top of the ridge, a cold wind blowing from the west, and driving a few plump grey clouds before it. It whipped up a succession of choppy little waves on the harbor, and bent the reeds in the swamps stretching away to the south. But Francis was hardly conscious of either weather or landscape—what he saw, in great relief, was the small battered brig swaying at her moorings directly below him.

***

Throughout that same afternoon, far from the town and the harbor, a ragged sandy-bearded man was working in the orchard of a farm near Campbelltown. Josiah Gracechurch had no fondness for hard labor, and he knew he was taking a big risk in thus exposing himself only a week after his escape. But Campbelltown was a reasonable distance from Windsor, and he could only hope that news of his disappearance from the Edgeleys' estate had not traveled so far. He had to have food, and some sort of shelter, for a night or two while he laid his plans.

The farm was a small, poorly-tended place, kept by an old Irishman and his daughter. Gracechurch felt sure that O'Connor was a ticket-of-leave man, as so many of the colonial Irish were, and Gracechurch pretended to be the same himself, to avoid any suspicion. Neither O'Connor nor his shabby overworked daughter seemed inclined to ask questions, however—they were grateful enough to find a hired hand who asked only for a bed in the barn, and a portion of food. They could not have paid him in any other currency.

At dinner-time that day, Miss O'Connor had been ready to talk a little with the only visitor they had had in many months, and Gracechurch had listened with steadily growing interest as she described her nearest neighbors, Mr. and Mrs. Rose.

"Such kind folks, they are," she said, stirring the strong black tea with the single spoon which her father and the laborer also shared. "Last time we took our wheat for grinding—it would have been nearly two months back—the Roses were looking after a whole crowd of children, nine or ten of them. They were all orphans, Mrs. Rose said, although there was a lady with them. She'd brought them all the way from England by herself."

Gracechurch took a great gulp of scalding tea to hide his excitement. With an effort, he asked casually:

"From England, you say? Maybe from London?"

"Somewhere in the Midlands, I think. We don't know England ourselves. Have you ever been to Enniskillen or thereabouts?" she added wistfully. "That's where our home was."

Gracechurch shook his head.

"I'm a Midlander too. I might know these children— that's why I asked. But it ain't important. They'd have gone from here now, I suppose."

"Yes, they stayed only a few days. They were traveling through to some place farther south—do you remember where it was, Father?"

The old man took a quick drink from his rum-bottle to refresh his memory, then pushed it across the table to Gracechurch.

"It was one of those blackfellow names," he said vaguely. "Something like Illywarry."

"It's a real lonely spot, they say," went on his daughter. "That lady must have had some spirit, setting out into the bush with a parcel of children. I often wonder whether they're all alive still."

With a heavy and lugubrious sigh, she stood up to clear away the dishes and feed the few scraps to the hens. Reluctantly Gracechurch put down the bottle and returned to his work.

As he hoed among the weed-choked trees, he told himself that he had had a real stroke of luck. He did not doubt that the Roses' visiting orphans were the emigrants from Switherby; after all, there could hardly be more than one such group, complete with middle-aged female guardian, in or about Sydney Town. He had a clear recollection of the party as he had seen it disembarking from the *Medway*

Queen, and Miss O'Connor's estimate of nine or ten children agreed with his own impression. Thus it seemed almost certain that his son and daughters were at present not far away at all, and could be found with little difficulty.

Gracechurch had thought a great deal about his offspring during his captivity, and his attitude towards them was practical rather than affectionate. His son would never be of much use, but the two girls would be of considerable value, both as housekeepers to their father, and later, as assets in the marriage market. Eligible females were scarce in the young community, and Gracechurch would drive a hard bargain when the time came.

But this was very much in the future, and for an escaped convict in a vast and inhospitable land, the future was uncertain, to say the least. He must get as far from Sydney as he could, yet at the same time he must not run the risk of losing himself utterly in the bush. Gracechurch now believed he had the ideal solution.

"I'll have to find my way somehow to this Illywarry," he reflected. "Shouldn't be too hard, if I'm careful. Then all I've got to do is take over this farm for myself, and live like a king. An old lady and a few boys won't be able to stop me. And seems it's too lonely a place for any troopers to come poking about. That's it—I'll be safe and cosy for the rest of my days!"

11

The First Runaway Comes Home

L UKE AND PAUL were fishing from the rocks on the south side of the little bay that ever since Eben's rescue of Mike had been known to them all as Bull-Calf Cove. It was an unromantic name, perhaps, but Gavin had been the first to use it, and Gavin was a solid and practical boy, and one whose opinion carried considerable weight. A favorite pastime of the older children, in their few leisure hours, was to draw maps of the area around the camp, and name the various physical features according to popular vote.

"Has the headland got a name yet?" Paul asked, dragging in his line for the tenth time to see whether the bait was intact.

"Cassie had some fancy-sounding thing, but nobody else liked it," said Luke. "I suppose by this evening she'll have thought of something else."

"If I caught the biggest fish in the sea, then we could call the cliff Cape Paul Brown, couldn't we? I should like to have my name on a map."

"All we need is one more decent-sized fish, then there'll be enough for dinner," said Luke, counting the catch that

146

lay in a pool beside him. "So never mind trying to hook a whale."

"Are whales fish?"

"They live in the sea, don't they?" retorted Luke, whose knowledge of natural history was slight. "So they must be fish."

For a few moments they sat in silence, watching their floats bobbing in the lazy blue-green swell. Then Paul said tenaciously:

"Octopuses live in the sea, too. Are they fish?"

"It doesn't matter what they are. It's no wonder you can't catch anything—you talk too much."

The next interval of quiet lasted almost five minutes, during which Luke had a bite, and lost it.

"I'm tired of eating fish, anyway," said Paul finally. "I hope Gavin has got another duck. Missabella is going to buy some hens in the summer—then we shall have eggs, and p'r'aps chicken sometimes."

"You can't have the eggs, and kill the hens too," Luke pointed out. "Wait till we start breeding pigs, and have pork and ham and bacon. It makes me hungry just to think of it."

"Did Missabella say we should have pigs?"

"Not exactly. She said we might, if we could afford them," admitted Luke, to whom the vigorous outdoor life was a tonic which raised his appetite to formidable proportions. "Here, give me a hand—I've got something."

He pulled in a blackfish of quite respectable size, and after stowing away their lines, the two boys set to work to clean their catch. Paul found this task rather distasteful, but like all the orphans, he had learned to endure what could not be cured. So he scraped and cut manfully, thankful when at last he could go down to the water's edge and wash the slippery fillets in the clean cold sea.

He was thus engaged when a lone figure appeared on the crest of the headland and began to descend towards the beach. Paul was partly hidden by the rocks, and he stayed cautiously where he was while he inspected the stranger. No other white person had ever been seen before on these shores by any of the children, and Paul was both surprised and curious.

"What are you staring at?" asked Luke, sliding down the rock to join him.

"There's a man coming," answered Paul, a little uncertainly, for he had suddenly had a peculiar and impossible thought about the approaching figure.

"It's not a man, it's a boy," said Luke. "He's carrying a bag—I expect he's been fishing, too."

"He can't have been fishing," declared Paul, standing up. "He *can't* have, because it's Francis."

Luke stood gaping while Paul raced across the sand and threw his arms around the newcomer's waist.

"It is, it is!" shouted Paul. "Come and see, Luke!"

But Luke could tell already that Paul was right. The weary, shabby, unkempt person was still recognizably Francis, taller and thinner, and in need of soap and water. Luke gathered up Paul's forgotten fish, and went to discover the why's and wherefore's.

"Have you brought us some stores from Sydney?" he asked hopefully, eyeing the sack which Francis had lowered thankfully on to the sand.

"He can't have come from Sydney, though," Paul said, looking puzzled. "Sydney's north, and he came the other way."

"I'll explain all about it, in a while," Francis said. "But I have to see Missabella first. Is it far to the farm?"

Paul pointed to the thickly-grown ridge behind the beach. "Just up there, only it doesn't look much like a farm yet. You'll be in good time for dinner—I'll let you have half my fish, and I'm sure Cassie will give you some of hers."

Francis shouldered his burden and followed his guides across the sand. How good it was to hear Paul's chatter again, and how well and sturdy he looked with his brown skin and thatch of sun-bleached hair! It had been a real stroke of luck to meet Paul and Luke like this, for often during the long hard trudge from Kiarmi —nothing but an uninhabited cove with a crude jetty built by the timber-cutters— Francis had despaired of ever seeing a familiar face again. He told the boys a little of his adventures as they scrambled up the bush track.

"There seems to be a native camp a few miles down the coast, near a big, queer, flat-topped rock. I think one of them saw me, and I was pretty frightened, but I thought the best thing to do was to keep on walking, and no one followed me."

"We have a black boy here," said Paul proudly, and he recounted the story of Cammy's journey from Sydney.

"He tells us where the best hunting-grounds are," added Luke. "And he climbs trees after *goannas*—you should see him! Only he's the only one who likes to eat them."

"One day I shall take you back to Kiarmi and show you the hole in the rocks where the water spouts up," said Francis, his weariness slipping away now that he was among friends. "It rushes through a sort of tunnel, and throws the spray yards into the air. Harry showed it to me before he went off to get the cedar."

They were approaching the clearing at last. Through the trees Francis could see the two crudely-built but solid huts, and before them the tilled ground of the vegetable garden. A rough post-and-rail fence now surrounded the entire cleared area on three sides; Eben and Gavin were at work on the fourth side, with Robin holding hammer and nails and twine. The twins were on duty as usual at the big stone fire-place in the middle of the clearing, while Selina was setting out the tin plates on a sawn-off tree-trunk which did double service as dining-table and carpenter's bench. Jessie and Mike, newly penned after their morning grazing, were dozing with every appearance of contentment.

Rosie the cat had smelt the fish as Luke stepped from the trees, and came to rub coaxingly against his bare legs. He was followed by Sally-Lou, draped in a holland apron liberally smeared with flour, for she had been helping Missabella mix the dough for the midday scone-loaf.

"Why is Francis here?" she demanded, in a clear cheerful voice that carried over the whole clearing.

The near-by hammering stopped, the cooks raised flushed and startled faces, and a wild-haired, wide-eyed figure dashed from one of the huts with a twig-fashioned broom in her hand.

"Francis!" exclaimed Cassie, with most unmaidenly loudness and vigor. "However did you come? Have you a holiday from school?"

She was crossing the clearing as she spoke, still clutching the broom, and now Missabella appeared, wondering at the commotion. Francis looked past Cassie at the shabby middle-aged woman, as neat and upright as ever, but seeming much older and thinner than Francis remembered, even after a brief two months. Francis had rehearsed to himself during the journey the speech he would make on this very occasion, and had thought himself word-perfect. However, confronted with his guardian he was seized by such pity and affection that he did what no one would have expected of the shy Francis—he ran forward and hugged her, and said nothing at all.

Cassie picked up the sack he had dropped, and began to examine its contents eagerly, as if it were the most natural thing in the world to find Latin grammars and history texts in the middle of the Illawarra. In unspoken agreement, the others went about their interrupted tasks, even the excited Paul, who withdrew to the fire-place to help Luke unload the morning's catch.

Alone in the hut with Missabella, Francis soon poured forth the story of his departure, not omitting the sale of his best clothes.

"But I thought if I worked hard here, and made things grow, perhaps one day I could earn some money to pay you back. Not just for the clothes, but for everything."

Missabella smiled then, sending Francis' hopes as high as the tree-tops.

"You shall never be asked to pay me back in money, Francis— not any of you. When I brought you here from Switherby, my one idea was to give you all a better chance in life than you had at home. If you take that chance, and use it well, then I am repaid in the best possible way. I *had* hoped to offer you the best chance of all, by providing you with a sound education."

"I know," said Francis, wishing he had his sister's gift of self-expression. "Only I just don't feel I was meant to be a scholar. I haven't that sort of mind."

"Then what do you mean to be? A runaway when things

go wrong?"

"No," Francis answered firmly. "I shall never run away from here, no matter what happens, because I want to be a farmer more than anything. I used to think about it even in Switherby, only it was no use talking of it there. Please—won't you just let me try?"

"I can hardly send you back at once, can I?" observed Missabella. "Not unless you walk. And I don't deny that we could do with another able-bodied boy on the place. Poor Gavin works like a galley-slave."

She patted Francis on the shoulder, and then with a return to her usual brisk no-nonsense manner, she said:

"As soon as you have eaten, you must write two letters of apology, one to Mr. Rose, and one to Mrs. Peachey, who must feel quite badly about your disappearance. In a few days I shall be sending Eben to Campbelltown for supplies, and he will take your letters."

"There's something else I have to tell you," said Francis, suddenly remembering Gracechurch. It no longer seemed so important, but Missabella took the news gravely enough.

"It may not be the same man, and even if it is, he cannot possibly know we are here. All the same, I shall tell Eben to keep a watch for any white strangers in the district. And don't mention this to the others, above all Robin and the two girls. They have quite forgotten their father, and I'm sure that is best in the circumstances."

Dinner that day was a gay and festive meal, although the fare was the same as usual. Francis was treated as the prodigal son, and all the choicest items of diet were offered to him.

"You may have *all* my cabbage," declared Sally-Lou, with a generosity that deceived no one, for her attitude towards the daily vegetable was one of whole-hearted loathing.

"Couldn't we grow lettuces, and silver beet, and broad beans?" asked Francis enthusiastically, surveying the kitchen-garden. "Harry says almost anything should grow here."

"You just try digging the ground first," said Gavin gloomily. "And keeping the birds and the insects away."

"In time, I hope we shall grow a great many things," Missabella said. "But it's winter, after all, and we cannot do too much until the spring. As long as we can provide ourselves with three meals a day, and keep warm and dry, we're doing very well indeed."

In spite of her calm words, she felt vaguely uneasy. The sun was bright, the wind gentle, and the young faces about her were rosy and happy. She surely need have no worries other than the usual everyday ones about money and the weather. Why, then, should she feel that another kind of threat was hanging over her little flock?

**

The next day was Sunday, according to the calendar that Cassie had made soon after their arrival in the Illawarra, working from the date of their departure from Mount Gilead. It was their sole means of distinguishing one day from the next; Missabella had insisted from the beginning that Sunday should be observed in a fitting manner, whatever their surroundings, but the other six days of the week were interchangeable.

"We don't have to work so hard on Sundays," Cassie explained to her elder brother over breakfast. "Jessie still has to be milked and taken to pasture, and the boys must still go out and catch our dinner, but we don't dig or hoe or make fences, and everyone has to have a bath before supper."

"Where?" asked Francis, looking around the tub-less clearing.

"In the sea, of course. It's cold, but it feels lovely afterwards. You will soon get used to it."

As the day wore on, Francis began to find the prospect of an afternoon dip quite inviting. The night had been crisp and chilly, the early morning touched with a cool sea-mist, but by midday the sun shone from a soft blue sky, transforming the clearing into a nest of warmth and stillness among the soaring trees.

"We have a short kind of Sunday service before dinner," Cassie said, emerging from the girls' hut with her hair newly brushed and her apron off. "There's only one hymn-book, so you must try and remember the words."

Francis associated hymns and prayers with churches and Sunday clothes, and at first he felt Missabella's brief little service to be rather incongruous in this setting, with a cow and a calf looking on, to say nothing of a horse and a cat, and with only the trodden earth to kneel upon. But when Cassie stood up to read the Psalm, he realized suddenly that the words had real meaning:

" 'I will lift up mine eyes unto the hills, from whence cometh my help. My help cometh from the Lord, which made heaven and earth.' "

Slightly removed from the little group of children stood Eben, and he, too, was listening intently, his grave blue eyes fixed upon Cassie. Beyond him the trees merged into velvety green ridges that rose to meet the mountain range on the western horizon, an outcrop so steep yet thickly wooded that it was like some gigantic dark wall between the pilgrims and the unknown world beyond.

" 'I will lift up mine eyes unto the hills'," Francis repeated to himself. "How wonderful that I should be here at last, and that I am to be allowed to stay! I shall see those hills every morning until I am an old man, and be glad."

The children had one favorite hymn to which even Sally-Lou knew the words, and they sang it now, with lusty cheerful voices and no accompaniment save the occasional cooing of wood-pigeons and the distant hum of the sea:

> "Who would true valor see,
> Let him come hither;
> One here will constant be,
> Come wind, come
> weather."

"It's a good song for us," said Cassie afterwards. "We're still pilgrims, aren't we, because our work isn't finished yet. Missabella says it will take years to turn this into a real farm, with a proper house and garden and fields for the cows."

"What about your lessons, though?" Francis asked, failing to see how his sister's restless vitality was to be satisfied by toil in the dairy or the orchard. "Aren't you going to do any more?"

"Missabella hasn't time to teach me, but now you've brought your books I shall work at them by myself. And I'm teaching Eben to read and write. He learns very quickly. Perhaps he will use your books, too."

Francis stared at her in surprise.

"Whatever for? What good would Latin or history be to a convict?"

Her reaction quite mystified him—she glowered at him as angrily as she had been wont to do during their childish arguments in the little home in Switherby.

"We don't even *think* of Eben as a convict any more. He works harder than any of us, and he's so kind—he'd never do anyone harm. And one day he will be free, and just as good as the next man, you'll see."

"All right," said Francis peaceably. "I believe you. You said you would show me the spring and the swamp. Can we go now?"

Cassie's mood changed again at once, and she ran to tell Missabella where they were going. The hours between dinner and bathing-time on Sundays were quite free, and the children could amuse themselves as they wished, provided they kept within calling-distance of home—for one of Missabella's continual fears was that someone might stray too far into the bush and fail to return.

Paul and Luke and the twins had gone to the shore with Gavin to search for shells, but Robin and Cammy abandoned their tree-climbing to accompany Francis and Cassie, and at the last minute Francis persuaded Selina to leave her embroidery and go with them too.

"Sally-Lou's having a nap, so we shan't have her to look after," said Cassie, with some relief, for minding the active and inventive baby of the family was not her favorite task. She rather wished that Francis had not invited Selina, either, for she felt that she had various private matters to discuss with her brother, but she had to admit that Selina was no longer such a boring companion. She had not mentioned the ancestral castle for weeks, and she was always willing to do Cassie's share of the washing and cleaning as well as her own.

"We had better take the buckets and bring back some water," Selina suggested now. "It's time to wash Sally-Lou's hair, and you can't do that in salt-water."

"Where did you get the extra buckets from?" Francis asked, studying the clumsy wooden contraptions.

"Eben makes them out of the trunks of the cabbage-palms," explained Cassie. "They leak a little, but when one wears out we just throw it away and get another one."

Robin and Cammy ran ahead down the steep shadowed track. Cassie would have liked to run with them, but Francis and Selina chose a more decorous pace, so for once Cassie decided to restrain herself. She did wonder, however, whether ladylike airs and graces would ever become her as they so easily became the fair Selina. Somehow it seemed rather unlikely.

***

Gracechurch was in an angry and desperate mood. His first self-congratulatory optimism had completely deserted him during the rough and difficult journey from Campbelltown; he had lived on roots and a few dubious berries, washed down by cold water. He wished he had had the foresight to bring old O'Connor's rum-bottle on his midnight departure from the farm, but he had not lingered long enough to attend to such details. At supper that same day Miss O'Connor had mentioned that troopers were in the district, looking for an escaped convict, and by morning her suspicions of Gracechurch could easily have been aroused. So here Gracechurch was, two days later, crouched among rocks on top of yet another scrubby ridge, weak from hunger and all the more savage because of it.

"How do you find any landmarks in this terrible country?" he asked himself, turning from a glimpse of the sea on his left hand to a partly-screened view of mountains on his right. "How do I know how many miles I've come? It seems like a hundred."

He stared down a lushly-clothed slope that was exactly like a dozen others he had recently traversed. Surely they were the same weird bunchy-topped palm-trees, the identical lacy ferns and shiny stiff-leaved shrubs he had pushed his weary way through this morning?

"You're getting weak in the head," he told himself scornfully. "Of course it's not the same. Because what you're looking at down there is water, a swamp, maybe. There would be fish, or eels."

He had no idea how he would catch such creatures with only his bare hands, but at least the swamp gave him an objective, and that was all he needed to revive his waning strength. As long as he kept walking, he would be warm, and able to ignore the tattered and useless state of his clothing.

He was skirting the swamp to the east when he heard the voices. At first he thought he might have gone out of his mind altogether, for the voices were raised in song, and in that limitless wilderness they seemed to come from the air itself. But as he listened, he heard, too, the crackling of twigs beneath what must certainly be human feet, and he had time to hide among a tangle of tree-ferns before the first figure came into view on the opposite hill-side.

"Well, I'll be—" he remarked silently. "It's a black boy. Got a spear, too, but he doesn't look big enough to be dangerous."

And then Gracechurch's surprise and gratification grew, and his confidence surged back. He hardly noticed the two girls and the half-grown lad who were all still singing as they came—what he saw, and rejoiced at, was the unmistakable figure of his own son.

"Now that's a piece of luck! You've been pretty clever after all, Joe Gracechurch! The bigger children are fetching water, so they must live close by. All I have to do is follow them."

His first impulse was to reveal himself at once, and confront Missabella with Robin as hostage. But he was shrewd enough to realize the need for caution. The orphans might be better protected than he knew, nor could he recall the sizes and strength of the older boys in the party. He was weak from hunger and exposure, and must rely on cunning as well as muscle.

Consequently, when Francis and his companions toiled back up the hill with the buckets, they were followed by Gracechurch at a respectful distance. Once Cammy stopped and turned, and stared down the darkening track, causing the intruder to drop hurriedly to his knees.

"What's the matter, Cammy?" asked Cassie. "Was it a wallaby?"

Cammy grinned, shook his head, and scrambled on towards the huts. He knew it was Sunday bathing-time, and he was anxious to join the other boys in the cold clear water of the cove—not because he cared about being clean, but because it was all such remarkable fun.

12

The Second Makes Trouble

"DON'T FORGET THE oatmeal, or the biscuits, or the new blade for the scythe," urged Missabella, standing shivering by the cattle-pen in the milky light of a winter dawn.

"And remember the sewing-thread I wanted," added Selina. "I wrote it down on the back of Missabella's list."

Francis hurried up with a bundle of letters and handed them to Luke, who sat behind Eben on Tomkins' broad and unruffled back. They were about to set forth on the long, hard ride to Campbelltown, and did not expect to return before the evening of the following day. It was Luke's first jaunt away from the farm, and he sat very erect, rigid with self-importance.

"I've left the gun with Gavin, Ma'am," said Eben. "He'll need it for hunting, and we shall be safe enough."

The listener hidden just beyond the clearing followed the brief conversation with avid interest. Fortune was certainly favoring Gracechurch lately. The only adult male in Missabella's group was departing, at a highly convenient time. Moreover, he had unwittingly revealed the existence of a gun and its whereabouts. Gracechurch had studied the topography of the clearing on the previous evening, and also had taken careful note of the number and physique of its inhabitants. The boy called Gavin had already attracted his attention, because of his obvious competence and responsibility. Gracechurch was not going to underestimate him, youthful though he was.

"Nobody else to be reckoned with, though, with the man out of the way," Gracechurch reflected now. "That other lad's a skinny bit of a thing, and the girls can't give any trouble."

He gazed at his two daughters, who were gathering up the breakfast dishes and washing them in a bucket. In the six or eight months since he had last seen them, they had somehow been transformed from pale, pudgy, sullen young creatures to a pair of rosy and cheerful and tolerably comely girls, and this pleased their father immensely, in view of his plans for their future.

"Won't they get a surprise when they see their long-lost father!" he observed to himself. "Well, they haven't long to wait."

During the night he had managed to take some milk and cheese from the shelves at the back of the girls' hut, and so was feeling quite invigorated. His prospects were beginning to seem as bright as the crimson-tipped clouds that hung over the quiet sea.

" 'Red at morning, shepherd's warning'," quoted Cassie, staring eastwards after the departed travelers. "Perhaps the weather is going to change. The jackasses have been laughing their heads off."

"You had better show me how to milk Jessie," suggested Francis. "Then I can do it while Eben's away."

They turned towards the pen, and so did not see the

figure emerging from the bush on the western edge of the clearing—that is, not until Robin suddenly began to scream. For a long moment everyone seemed frozen like statues in their various poses, from Paul and Sally-Lou in the vegetable garden to Missabella at the fire-place.

"Who is it?" whispered Cassie, appalled at the tall, unshaven, unwashed, and half-clad apparition. "Is it a white man?"

But Francis knew at once who it was. He recalled Edgeley's description of the big convict with the sandy beard, and it fitted, now that the man had moved into the patch of pale sunlight in the center of the clearing. Clearly this was Gracechurch, and Francis did not for a minute believe that his mission was friendly.

"It's Robin's father, isn't it?" Cassie said, certain that only such an encounter could upset Robin so completely. "He must have been one of the convicts on our ship, after all."

By this time Missabella had moved to meet the intruder, who grasped his son in one hand and kept the other fist menacingly clenched.

"What do you want?"

As Missabella spoke with all her considerable dignity, Francis noted that Gavin was moving slowly towards the huts, in one of which the gun was kept. But Gracechurch had been waiting for this, and in a few strides he had reached the doorway and barred Gavin's entry.

"You'd better let me have the gun," he said. "It's not safe for a lad like you to be meddling with fire-arms."

He released Robin and dived into the shadows of the hut, to emerge with the musket held confidently at the ready.

"I'm going to be in charge here now, and I can prove it with this 'ere weapon, see? So all of you be sensible and don't go running no risks."

Missabella, holding the weeping Robin in her arms, sat down abruptly on the sawn-off stump. Silently the other children gathered around her, the twins keeping as far from their father as they possibly could.

"You must do as he says," Missabella told them all sternly. "I don't know what he wants, but whatever it is we must stay together and keep calm."

"I don't want much," remarked Gracechurch. "Just a bite of food and some shelter, and my own children about me. You won't deny, Ma'am, that I have a right to them?"

"I do deny it," said Missabella steadily. "You deserted them months ago, and before that you ill-treated your family for years."

"They're still my children, and not yours."

Missabella remained silent, knowing that in the legal sense Gracechurch was quite right. It had not seemed necessary legally to adopt any of the Switherby orphans; she had no idea whether, as a convict, Gracechurch had forfeited his claims to his offspring. In any case, she had no intention of arguing legal points with an armed and dangerous ruffian. Somehow she had to fight her rising panic and discover a means of outwitting him.

"This is a fine bit of property you've got here," the convict went on. "You need a man about the place to see to things, though."

"We have Eben," Cassie burst out. "We don't need *you*."

Gracechurch studied her with an angry scowl.

"You'd best speak when you're spoken to, and not before. I know your precious Eben isn't here, and I know where he's gone. By the time he gets back I'll be well and truly the master, here, and he'll do what I say."

He glanced along the row of frightened young faces. "Where's the black boy? You, Martha, tell me where he's gone."

But Martha could only stammer again and again that she did not know, and Marianne came bravely to her rescue.

"None of us has seen him. He goes hunting early in the morning."

"I s'pose it doesn't matter much," her father grunted. "A little black like that couldn't do me any harm. Now then, all of you, get about your work, only don't go out of sight."

"The cow and calf must be taken to graze near the beach," Missabella pointed out. "Otherwise they have no food."

"You and one of the young ones can go, then. I reckon you'll understand that if you try to get help, the children you've left behind will surely suffer."

For a moment Missabella stared at him intently, as if measuring the depths of his malevolence. She must have decided it was quite profound, for she turned away, saying:

"We have no neighbors. There will be no need to harm the children."

"How can she give in so easily?" demanded Cassie, as she and Francis went to fetch hoes and spades. "Does she really mean to let that awful man stay here on our own farm? He might be here for weeks."

"I think that's what he hopes," said Francis gloomily. "What can Missabella do? He's big and strong, he has the gun, and there's no help for miles. It could even be years before any troopers catch up with him."

Cassie tightened her grip on the hoe as the full implications of the convict's presence dawned upon her. He had arrived so suddenly and utterly without warning that at first his coming had seemed like part of a dream. Even Robin's terror had had a remote and unreal quality, like a child's fright at a nightmare. But now Gracechurch had become solid and dimensional, and Cassie had to realize that there was no escaping from him in reality, as one could escape so readily from a dream.

"Eben will be back tomorrow," she said desperately.

"What can he do? It would be dangerous if he tried to attack Gracechurch. Besides, Eben is a convict himself—"

"He's not a bit like this man!" cried Cassie. "Eben would never do anything to hurt us. And he never thinks about escaping, I know. He has no family but us."

"All right, supposing that's true, and Eben does try to get rid of Gracechurch. What do you think Gracechurch wants the gun for?"

"You mean, he would really shoot Eben?"

"He might. Gracechurch couldn't get himself into any worse trouble than he's in now, no matter how much shooting he does."

Cassie dug her hoe blindly into a clump of weed.

"He mustn't, Francis. We have to warn Eben somehow."

"I'm not just trying to frighten you," Francis said, more gently. "But you have to know what sort of a man Gracechurch is. Missabella knows, that's why she's not doing anything to make him angry. And if you speak out the way you did a few minutes ago, *you* might make him lose his temper. We have to be sensible and try to think of something really clever."

"You think of it, then," said Cassie crossly. "I'm going to hoe as hard as I can and pretend these weeds are that man Gracechurch. Why did he have to come and spoil everything?"

After this childish outburst she felt a little calmer, and worked on steadily. From time to time she or Francis glanced around to see how the others were faring. Selina was showing unexpected coolness in the face of imminent danger, and quietly went about her laundering without as much as a tremor, although Gracechurch had evidently noticed her fair prettiness and was showing an unpleasant interest in her. The twins were naturally still greatly upset, and could only keep close together and try to remember the details of their daily tasks. Paul and Sally-Lou were too bewildered to do anything but potter about near the huts, making sure Missabella was not far away.

Missabella had trained herself long ago to conceal her feelings, for she believed that to display them openly was undignified in the extreme. Such discipline aided her now, for she was able to remain cool and collected in front of both Gracechurch and the children, while her fearful and anxious mind went over and over the possibilities of outwitting this dreadful man and restoring all her brood to safety. Like Francis, she realized that any plan would have to be most carefully and cunningly executed, without any risk whatsoever to the children or to Eben. Meanwhile, the flock must be fed.

"We have no meat or fish for dinner," she said to Gracechurch. "Surely you can trust two of the boys to go and catch something for us."

"I'll go meself," said the convict. "I'll take the gun, and that big lad will come and help me. And young Robin can go with us. It'll be the worse for him if any of you try to make off while we're gone."

Robin shrank away at the sound of his name, and clutched Missabella's skirts, but she gently detached the clinging hands, trying all the while to make him understand why he must accompany his father. The child was too confused and frightened to respond, and had finally to be lured away by Gavin with promises of a ride on his back.

"Francis, Paul and I will take the cow and calf down to the beach," Missabella said, trying not to watch Robin's small figure limping out of sight. "You and Cassie must look after Sally-Lou while Marianne and Martha see to the fire and the cooking. And please remember, Cassie, to do nothing foolish or dangerous, or we may all suffer."

"I do believe she can read people's thoughts," said Cassie gloomily, when Missabella had departed. "But it's not dangerous to make plans, is it, when Gracechurch can't hear us?"

"You said you couldn't think of anything," Francis reminded her, automatically removing Sally-Lou to a safe distance from the fire. A gun-shot from the direction of the swamp told them of the hunters' whereabouts, so certainly Gracechurch could not hear their discussion.

"I know, but something occurred to me a few minutes ago," said Cassie. "It's no use trying to get a message to Eben, because Gracechurch will be expecting us to do that, and it would be too risky. But there could be help even closer than that."

Francis had to admit that once again his sister's mind was moving too quickly for him. He frowned at the toes of his sadly scuffed shoes.

"Where? Surely Mount Gilead is the closest? Only one man lives at the Five Islands."

"Can't you see? It's only two days since you came down from Sydney with Harry—won't their ship still be in that harbor you spoke of?"

"Kiarmi," said Francis absently. He needed more time to think this out.

"Well, that's not far, is it?"

"About two hours' walk, perhaps more. But Harry and the others will be in the bush cutting timber."

"Of course they will—I thought of that," said Cassie impatiently. "Only they wouldn't leave their ship deserted, would they? Someone would have to stay on board, and that person would know where the others had gone."

Francis transferred his gaze from his shoes to his sister's flushed and eager face, and his glance held a certain respect.

"That's quite true. And there are half a dozen men besides Harry—all big fellows. Some of them have guns."

"And they'll all have axes," added Cassie, with grim satisfaction. "They would soon drive Gracechurch away for good. Francis, we just *have* to fetch them."

"How?" asked Francis. "Gracechurch would soon miss one of us in the daytime, and we could never find our way to Kiarmi in the dark. I know, because you have to follow the beaches, and climb over rocks and cliffs."

"There's one person Gracechurch won't miss, someone he hasn't really seen yet, except that first time at the spring."

"You mean Cammy? But where is he?"

"That's just the trouble," said Cassie with a sigh. "We don't know. But we must find him, without Gracechurch knowing."

***

Cammy had been out hunting when Gracechurch made his entrance into the camp. Sometimes Robin accompanied his friend on these expeditions, but on this particular morning Cammy had indicated, in his usual sign-language, that he intended to try and kill a snake, and Robin loathed such reptiles, dead or alive, so Cammy set off alone. He had crossed the swamp by his own private path which the others could never follow, and spent a happy hour or two prowling through the dense scrub beyond. A hibernating snake was not the easiest thing to find in this jungle, but Cammy had endless patience and no consideration of time, and eventually he met with success in the shape of a comatose brown reptile of satisfactory length and plumpness. Cammy dispatched it with practiced rapidity, and turned homeward, trailing the corpse behind him.

He was about to re-cross the swamp when he heard a shot. Cammy had a deep instinctive mistrust of fire-arms, an attitude which persisted in spite of Gavin's attempts to teach him that a gun, properly handled, need not be feared. Cammy liked to keep at a safe distance from the hunting-party whenever the musket was in use, and so now he crouched down among the tough-bladed grasses while he gauged the white people's whereabouts.

Expecting to see Gavin and one or two of the other children, he was surprised and puzzled to observe a stranger. Large and bearded and oddly menacing, he stood at the eastern edge of the swamp, watching while Gavin retrieved the bird he had just shot. Behind him, barely visible but to Cammy immediately recognizable, was Robin.

Intuition bade Cammy stay where he was. Presently Gavin returned, and the stranger directed him further along the swamp. Robin slipped on the muddy reeds, and at once the big man rounded on him with upraised fist and a few angry words which Cammy could not hear, but whose threat he could positively feel. Nor did his keen eyes miss Robin's terrified shrinking from that large looming figure.

Cammy could sense that something was wrong, certainly. His affection for Robin gave him an urge to rush out and defend the child, but a more primitive emotion soon succeeded it. The ways of the white man were still strange and bewildering to Cammy, no matter how much he enjoyed sharing the life of the orphans on the hill-top. Their ways were not yet completely his, nor could their notions of right and wrong ever become quite clear to him. He did not know this other white man, nor could he predict what the stranger's attitude towards himself would be, therefore he, Cammy, would wait and watch until the whole situation clarified itself.

In the meantime he was hungry, so he set to work to roast his snake. To do this he took the precaution of retiring several hundred yards to the south-west, in the opposite direction to that which the white people had taken, so that the sight and smell of smoke might not attract too much attention. Patiently he rubbed two sticks together until he had a spark—how much simpler it was with Missabella's magical flints!—and set fire to the driest twigs and pieces of bark that he had been able to find. Then he had to wait until the flames had died down before he could toss on the skinned snake, and while it was cooking he squatted on a rock and thought of nothing in particular. One activity at a time was enough for Cammy.

The snake was rich and satisfying, and afterwards Cammy curled up near the dwindling fire and slept for a while. When he awoke the sun had disappeared behind the purpling mountains, and a penetrating chilly mist was creeping over the swamp.

Cammy knew it was time to go back to the evening warmth and friendliness of the camp, but he was still uneasy about the big stranger's presence. So he traveled cautiously and slowly, keeping always to the shelter of the scrub, and making no sound. Thus he reached the edge of the clearing just as the early June dusk descended, and knowing he could not be seen, he sat down with his spear across his knees and made his observations.

As his eyes became accustomed to the dimness, he made out the shapes of his friends at their supper around the fire. At first sight everything seemed normal enough; Missabella presided over the plates and cups, the girls helped serve and hand round, even Rosie was in his usual place at Sally-Lou's feet, waiting for scraps. Beyond in the cattle-pen, Jessie sighed and blew as she chewed her cud. It was all so quiet that Cammy could distinctly hear the crooning of the waves on the hidden shore.

And it was the silence that troubled him. Supper-time was usually an occasion for happy chatter and laughter and the exchanging of plans for the next day. Sometimes Selina, who had the best and sweetest voice of the group, would sing a solo, and later all the children would join in some familiar chorus. This Cammy greatly enjoyed. But tonight no one even spoke until the meal was finished, and then the first voice was that of the stranger.

"Haven't you got any candles? You there, Martha, fetch a bit of light!"

Cammy had been with the group long enough to become accustomed to their way of addressing one another, and the man's harshness and rudeness was new and unpleasant. When the candles were brought, Cammy noticed, too, the stranger's ugly manner of eating; he leaned well forward over the make-shift table, shoveling food into his mouth with both hands, disposing of any scraps that may have been left when the others finished. Cammy saw the figure of Missabella moving away from the table, and if anyone's bearing could register distaste and dislike, then hers certainly did.

One by one the children retired to the huts and early bed, and again the lack of noise was distinctly odd. Usually Cammy slept in his own crude but well-loved shelter near the cattle-pen, and more than once Cassie glanced in that direction, but tonight it was to remain empty. Cammy intended to stay as far as possible from the frightening newcomer with the unkempt beard and savage tongue. When at length Gracechurch stretched himself out in the doorway of the boys' hut, with the gun beside him, Cammy slipped off into the bush, to the company of the possums and wallabies and birds, whose ways he could readily understand.

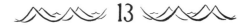 13

Cammy Goes South

"PLEASE, PLEASE, MAKE Cammy come," Cassie whispered imploringly to the overcast sky. "He must come *soon.*"

During the night the weather had changed abruptly with the arrival of a strong south-west wind, and now rain was threatening. Already a curtain of grey showers had come down over the horizon, and the beach was a desolate, chilly place, swept by the wind and encroached upon by mounting metal-colored waves. Cassie and Francis had brought Jessie and Mike to graze, and although they were relieved enough to leave the gloomy, unhappy atmosphere of the camp, they were both despondent and subdued.

"If the weather changes, Harry's timber-gang might decide to go on to the Shoalhaven," Francis said pessimistically. "There's more shelter there, I remember Harry saying so."

"They can't set sail if a gale comes up," Cassie pointed out, surveying the southern headland where the foam was being tossed ever higher against the cliff. "And it's going to rain."

"They can't cut timber if the rain's too heavy," Francis observed.

"Then they shall probably go back to the ship, and today will be just the time to find them," said Cassie. "Couldn't you pretend I'd got lost for a few hours, long enough to walk to Kiarmi and fetch Harry?"

"Don't you think Gracechurch would realize you were up to something? He's quite clever, you know."

Cassie nodded, and sighed. Francis was right, of course. But how unbearably wretched it was, to sit about and do nothing to help, while Gracechurch lorded over the camp as if it were really his! Missabella looked so sad and anxious, and she had hardly eaten anything at breakfast, while Robin was so bowed and lifeless that he seemed like a little old man. Would their cheerful hopeful community ever be the same again?

"We'd better bring Mike back," said Francis. "He's too close to the water."

They crossed the pale sand to the headland where Mike had found a patch of grass much to his undeveloped taste. From the ridge they could look down into the next bay, and Cassie paused to watch a dozen crabs scuttling over the rocks.

"Silly things," she said. "What are they all running about for?"

Even as she gazed, she had her answer, for from under a ledge a short black arm thrust an accurate spear, and the biggest crab was well and truly impaled.

"Cammy!" cried Cassie, so loudly that Francis ran to her side in alarm. "Cammy, come out!"

"S'sh!" urged Francis. "Gracechurch might be watching, for all we know. Is it really Cammy?"

"It *has* to be," said Cassie, with such fervor that her brother was almost convinced of the existence of miracles. "He'll come out in a minute."

It was more like five minutes, however, before Cammy crawled out from beneath his rock, with the crab still attached to his spear. He approached very cautiously, glancing all around the beach and scanning the backdrop of bush before he assured himself that the brother and sister were truly alone.

"What's the matter, Cammy?" Francis asked. "Why don't you come back to the camp?"

Cammy dropped his spear and made exaggerated signs to depict a large figure with a beard and clenched fists. He then waved in the direction of Mount St. Matthew, and shook his head most emphatically.

"However can we make him understand?" Francis said despairingly. "It will take hours."

But Cassie could display extraordinary patience when she saw the need for it, and she now set to work to explain in words and pictures what Gracechurch was doing. She was shrewd enough to stress the man's cruelty towards Robin; at this point Cammy's eyes widened, and his hand reached instinctively for his spear.

"Big man has gun," Cassie said. "He might shoot. You get help."

She repeated this several times, then led Cammy down to the wet sand at the water's edge. Here she drew a picture of a sailing-ship, another of two or three men with axes, and finally a sketch of Cammy himself, handing a piece of paper to one of the men.

"That way," she said, pointing south. "Near flat-topped rock. Ki-ar-mi."

Cammy may or may not have recognized the native name, but he nodded at the mention of the flat rock, which was a landmark known to him from his fishing expeditions. After Cassie had led him through the sequence of drawings once again, he grinned and held out his hand, pointing to the oblong which represented the message he was to carry.

Francis gave a long sigh of relief. So far, so good. From one pocket he produced a stubby piece of pencil, and from another Cassie's letter, which he had carried from Sydney.

"Just as well I have only one jacket now," he observed. "I'd better write the note, because Harry knows me best."

While he carefully printed every word—he was not too sure of Harry's reading ability, but surely someone in his party would be literate—Cassie made certain that the rising tide hid every vestige of her sand-drawings. It would never do for Gracechurch to discover them. Meanwhile, Cammy unconcernedly pulled his crab apart and ate it raw—he realized he would not have time to cook it.

As Francis completed the message, the rain began to fall, softly at first, but steadily enough to suggest more than a passing shower. Cammy tucked the paper into the waistband of his ancient trousers, and buttoned up the over-large waistcoat which was his sole upper garment. In a moment of inspiration, Francis removed his own peaked cap and placed it on the native boy's head. Cammy had a fondness for headgear of any kind, and his pleased smile was so broad that it seemed like a break in the clouds. Without more ado he took his spear and jogged off over the headland.

"I hope he remembers what he has to do," said Francis anxiously.

"Will Harry realize he doesn't mean any harm?" wondered Cassie. "I should have told him to put down his spear before he went near the white people. Oh, well, it's too late now."

They watched the dwindling oddly-clad figure until it was lost to sight in the mists of rain. At last, shivering and reluctant, they rounded up Jessie and her calf, and turned towards what no longer felt like home.

***

The afternoon and night that followed were the longest Cassie had ever known. With the rain pouring incessantly on the palm-leaf roof, the children huddled in the huts, keeping close together for warmth, and watching for any leaks. Earlier, Gavin and Francis had rigged a rough shelter for the fire-place, but the rain was driving beneath it and hissing malevolently upon the ashes. Gracechurch sat hunched near the doorway, the gun in his lap, occasionally swearing at the weather or demanding more blankets to add to the collection he had already appropriated. Once he shouted across to Missabella:

"What time is that convict fellow due back?"

But in no circumstances was Missabella prepared to raise her voice to an unmannerly pitch. Instead, she sent Cassie scuffling over to the other hut with a verbal message to the effect that the rain had probably delayed the travelers until the next morning.

"Tell the missus she'd better not be trying to trick me," growled Gracechurch. "And what about some supper?"

A cold and cheerless meal was put together and eaten by candle-light, for darkness came soon after five on such a dreary evening. In the girls' hut the gloom was relieved a little when Cassie, at Missabella's instigation, began to relate one of her stories, an elaborate tale to which even Selina listened with desperate attention. Rosie the cat came dashing in from the rain-heavy blackness, and crept under Sally-Lou's blanket. With the candles throwing wavering shadows on the walls, and the roofing stoutly resisting the onslaught of the weather, the hut was cosy and friendly, and there was at least the illusion of security. But Cassie, even as she wove her network of words, was always aware of that threatening presence a few yards distant, and remembering Cammy trudging across the sand with Francis' cap on his head and an urgent message stuck in his waistband.

In the boys' hut, the atmosphere was hardly conducive to peaceful rest. Gracechurch, bored and chilled, had rummaged among the stores and found a half-bottle of spirits which Missabella kept for medicinal purposes. This discovery delighted him, and as the level in the bottle gradually sank, his mood grew more and more convivial, so that he insisted on the boys' staying awake to keep him company.

"Let's have a song!' he demanded. "What about 'Botany Bay'? You all know that, I'll be bound. One, two, three—come on, now!"

Francis and Gavin made a determined effort to humor their unwelcome guest, for both were old enough to see that his temper could readily alter for the worse if he were crossed, but Paul and Robin were too sleepy and confused to do anything except lie blinking in their corners.

"That boy isn't singing," declared Gracechurch, pointing at Robin. "Get up and give us a song on your own, or else you'll be sorry."

"Robin can't sing," Gavin said. "He can't remember the words."

"Then he'll learn them," said the convict viciously. "Just stubborn, that's what he is. I'll show him."

He reached across and pulled Robin upright, with a shake that made the child's head jerk violently. Robin opened his mouth, but not even the faintest semblance of words would come.

"Do something, quick," Gavin whispered urgently to Francis. "His father might kill him."

"Why don't we have a game of something instead of singing?" Francis asked in a moment of inspiration. "There's a checker-board, and we could use pebbles for pieces."

"That's a game for babies," grumbled Gracechurch, but nevertheless he released Robin and sat down in the middle of the floor, keeping both gun and bottle handy.

Paul was making a collection of stones from the beach, and this Francis raided hurriedly to provide men for the strange protracted game that followed. Gracechurch seemed prepared to stay awake all night; Francis and Gavin took turns as his opponent, struggling to keep their eyes open and to remain alert enough to satisfy him.

"You play a fair game," Gracechurch remarked once to Francis with a grudging admiration. "It's a pity I couldn't have had a clever sort of boy for a son, instead of that there miserable creature."

After this he sat in silence, brooding alternately over the checker-board and the almost-empty bottle, until finally he slumped backwards and began to snore. Only then did Francis and Gavin deem it safe to retire to their own blankets.

"Do you think he'll stay here forever?" Gavin whispered. "If only we could grab the gun?"

"He'd be awake the minute you touched it," Francis said.

"Let's go to sleep—things might be better in the morning."

This was a vague sort of comfort to Gavin, but Francis was fervently hoping that his words might be true. He slept fitfully, tormented by anxiety over Cammy—so many things could have gone wrong, and Cammy was only a small native boy, whose mind did not see matters from the white man's point of view. Cammy might simply ignore this mission if any worthwhile distraction crossed his path, or if he failed to find the timber-cutters immediately, he might take to the bush and not be seen again. When at last Francis slept, he dreamt feverishly of a Gracechurch grown to giant-size, playing checkers with pieces as big as the rocks on the beach . . .

He awoke to a dim, dripping world of cold mist, to a morning so bereft of light that it seemed just another dusk. Yet a glance at his beloved old watch—which instinct had told him to keep well concealed from Gracechurch—showed him that it was already eight o'clock.

"Aren't we going to have any breakfast?" asked Paul, who was dressed after a fashion, but afraid to stir out of the hut in case he roused the still-sleeping Gracechurch.

"Of course. Is Robin awake?"

"I don't know," said Paul. "He won't answer when I speak to him."

Francis gazed anxiously at Robin's pale un-childish face, wondering if the boy was ill, but it was fear that caused his silence and apathy—it seemed to Francis that if Gracechurch stayed much longer, what small vitality Robin had would vanish altogether, leaving just an empty shell.

"I'll go and help with the breakfast," Francis decided. "Then I'll bring some in for him. You wake Gavin."

When he stepped out into the clearing, the cold wet air

seemed to cling to his face and clothing, and he could barely see the trees at the edge of the vegetable patch. Away on his left a bulky shape moved and mooed in gentle protest—Jessie had not yet been milked. Francis roused Cassie and the twins, and set to work to make a fire from the few pieces of dry kindling that he could find.

"Nobody even wants to do any work any more," lamented Cassie. "What's the use, when we're only working for *him*?"

"Don't make too much noise," urged Francis. "He's still asleep, and the longer he sleeps, the better. Who's going to milk Jessie?"

"I suppose I will," said Cassie. "The twins have to get the porridge—I'm no good at it."

She took up the pail and slithered across the muddy ground to the pen. As it turned out, her decision to do the milking was a most fortunate one. Both Marianne and Martha would have been frightened out of their wits by the apparition which loomed from the fog on the far side of the railing. Even Cassie was momentarily so alarmed that she dropped her pail, and Mike started careering round his yard in alarm.

"Who's that?" a deep voice demanded. "Where's Francis?"

The figure in the mist seemed to Cassie's sleepy eyes to be of quite monstrous proportions, until common sense assured her that it was simply a tall man in a high-crowned hat, with his coat-collar turned up around his throat, and an axe held over one shoulder.

"Harry!" exclaimed Cassie in what was a subdued sort of sob.

"It's young Cassie, isn't it?" observed Harry, peering over the rail. "A little blackfellow gave me an odd kind of message—I thought I'd best see what was up."

"Thank goodness you came!" breathed Cassie. "I'll fetch Francis—just you stay there."

"Don't be too long," said Harry. "There's three of us, and we ain't had our breakfast yet."

But when Francis arrived, and he and his sister between them related the story of Gracechurch's arrival and his threat to the little settlement, Harry seemed to forget his hunger. Two more stalwart axe-bearing figures now leant on the rail beside him; one of them, after listening to the Browns' account, remarked indignantly:

"Lots of us may have been lags once, but we don't hold with stealin' from women an' little 'uns. Where is this feller?"

"He has a gun," warned Francis, pointing to the hut where Gracechurch presumably still slept.

"This fog could be a help," said Harry thoughtfully. "We could close up on the hut from behind. Can you get the other children out of the way?"

"I think so," and Francis, followed by Cassie, hurried back to acquaint Missabella and the others of their coming deliverance.

"I can hardly believe it," said Missabella wonderingly, but already the light of battle was returning to her dark-ringed eyes. "Be quick, Francis—make all the children go into the girls' hut and stay there."

Gavin and Paul had emerged at last, and reported that Gracechurch seemed to be still asleep.

"Robin hasn't moved, either," added Gavin. "Shall I bring him out?"

Glancing around, Missabella saw that Harry and his henchmen were slowly edging through the trees towards the back of the clearing. The fog had begun to lift a little, and time was precious.

"Hurry, then. Just pick him up and carry him."

But Gracechurch's brandy-induced sleep had not been as sound as they had hoped. Some instinct had told him to seize the gun as he awoke, and he loomed now in the doorway, so angry and threatening that Gavin instantly retreated.

"What's happening?" bellowed the convict. "Where is everybody?"

Missabella, Gavin, and Francis stood motionless as Harry and one of his mates crept round two opposite corners of the hut. Gracechurch hesitated for a fraction of a minute too long before raising his gun—he could not aim in two directions at once. Harry had the weapon in his own hand while Gracechurch was still attempting to size up the situation.

But somehow his luck held. For at that very moment Robin stumbled across the floor of the hut, bewildered by the sudden commotion, and his father's quick wits did not desert him. He snatched up the child, and backed towards the bush with Robin held before him as a shield.

"Give up, Gracechurch, you'll never get away!" Harry cried, lowering the now useless gun.

Gracechurch was not prepared to stay and argue. He dodged into the shelter of the trees, and almost immediately was lost to view, although the sound of his progress was loud enough to the stricken watchers.

"He's going towards the beach," said Francis. "Why don't we go after him?"

"We will, my lad, never fear," said Harry grimly, for he was a soft-hearted fellow, and he had seen only too clearly Robin's terrified face, and the bare misshapen legs beneath the child's pitifully inadequate nightshirt. "But we have to think this out—we can't risk harmin' the boy."

Despite her shock, Missabella had rapidly regained her organizing ability, and her alert eyes had seen at least one source of help.

"Cammy," she said abruptly. "He must have followed you back. Bring him here, Francis."

Cammy sidled up warily, his black eyes peering at Harry and the other men from under the rain-sodden peak of Francis' cap. If he was exhausted by his travels, he showed no signs of it.

"Bad man take Robin," said Missabella carefully. "You find which way, and tell us."

Cammy nodded, but his gaze had swivelled towards the fireplace where the twins' porridge-pot was beginning to bubble invitingly. On the whole Cammy did not fancy white people's food; now, however, he was so hungry that any form of nourishment appealed to him.

"Tell first, food afterwards," said Missabella firmly, and Cammy melted into the fog.

In a very few minutes the clearing sprang into life, as the other children came forth demanding explanations, and Missabella assigned duties all round. Until Cammy returned, Robin's rescue could not be tackled, and in the meantime the strength of Harry and his friends must be fortified with a quick but substantial breakfast. Over this they discussed ways and means of retrieving Robin—the capture of Gracechurch was now a secondary consideration—and to this council of war both Gavin and Francis were admitted. Cassie's job was the still urgent one of milking poor distracted Jessie.

"Put out some porridge for Cammy, so he can eat as soon as he comes back," Missabella told Martha, who like her twin was red-eyed with crying. "And try not to worry about

Robin—your father doesn't know the country, and can't get far."

She hoped silently and fervently that she was right. By now Gracechurch must be a very desperate man indeed, and it was useless to predict what he would do when cornered. Robin's safety hung very delicately in the balance, unless Gracechurch had decided to abandon him in order to make more rapid progress.

But Cammy returned without direct news of the boy. He had seen neither him nor his father; from their tracks, however, he was certain that they were heading south along the beach.

"Good," said Harry with satisfaction, replacing his hat and seizing his axe. "As long as he stays on the sand, we can follow him easily. And he won't take to that there jungle if he can help it."

"If it's a question of letting the man go and saving the child, then Gracechurch must be allowed to escape," said Missabella anxiously. "I'm sure he'll not bother us again."

"If he only knew it, he'd be better off in prison than wanderin' in that scrub," remarked Harry. "You could be lost there for fifty years and never set eyes on a livin' soul. Don't fret, Ma'am—we'll bring back the boy."

They set off briskly, Cammy proudly leading the way, and Gavin in the rear, carrying the musket. Francis went too, being classed as an able-bodied man, and Cassie watched him wistfully as he marched purposefully past the cattle-pen. She knew she should not regard the expedition as an adventure when Robin's life was at stake, but at least she could wish once again to be a boy, permitted to take part in the larger dramas and not forever relegated to the regions backstage.

14

Pilgrims on a Picnic

SEVERAL WEEKS LATER, when life at Mount St. Matthew had resumed a more or less normal course, Cassie persuaded Missabella to let all the children go on an excursion to Kiarmi. In fact, a reasonable excuse for a picnic was at hand—it happened to be Selina's birthday, according to the home-made calendar. But Cassie's real reason for wanting to go to Kiarmi was totally unconnected with celebrations; she wanted to visit the exact spot where the final events in the Gracechurch episode had taken place.

"I know you told us everything," she said to Francis. "Only I'd like to see for myself. Anyway, you said once before that you'd show us the hole where the water flies up in the air."

"I don't feel like having a picnic so close to where it all happened," protested Francis. "If you'd been there you would know what I mean."

"We can eat our dinner somewhere else, and visit the blowhole thing afterwards. You won't even have to look at it if you don't want to."

When the more gentle Selina added her pleas to Cassie's, Francis soon gave in. After all, it was a beautiful cloudless day, and he had been working very strenuously during the past weeks, bent on proving to Missabella that he was far more suited to farming than to studying.

Gavin, however, was absorbed in the manufacture of a real table for the girls' hut, and elected to stay with Missabella. At the last minute the latter decided Eben, too, had earned a holiday, and sent him off with the others, armed with sundry instructions concerning the safety of the smaller children. Cammy needed no urging to join the party, and even took a portion of cold roast *goanna* as his contribution to the feast.

"Poor Eben will have to carry Sally-Lou all the way home," said Cassie. "She should have stayed behind, but Missabella is not as good at saying 'no' to Sally as to the rest of us."

"I suppose, in a way Sally-Lou is really Missabella's own," observed Francis thoughtfully. "She's been with Missabella since she was born, and we were all taken in at the vicarage when we were half-grown."

"It doesn't make much difference, does it?" asked Marianne. "We'd none of us choose to be anyone else's children now."

"Selina might," said Cassie mischievously. "She might still like to be heiress to that grand estate somewhere-or-other."

But Selina was learning that teasing is often an odd by-product of affection, and she refused to be provoked. In any case, there was not enough truth in Cassie's words to warrant a reply—Selina had her place in a real close-at-hand family, and had gradually ceased to dream of her aristocratic but hopelessly remote relatives.

"Now that I'm twelve, I'm to think a little about my future," she said solemnly, for one attribute she had not lost was her precise manner of speaking. "Missabella told me so, at breakfast. In a year or two I may go to Sydney to be apprenticed to a good dressmaker."

"Can girls be apprentices?" asked Martha doubtfully.

"Whatever you do call them, then. And one day I might have my own shop, and design ball-dresses and bonnets and ever such finery."

"Cassie must be your first customer," declared Francis.

"Who wants ball-dresses?" asked Cassie scornfully. "And anyway, where should I get the money to pay for them? If I do any work at all, I shall probably have to go out as a governess, and they're as poor as mice, I'm sure. If I *do* have money to spend, I shall buy books, so there."

"You and Selina seem to have your lives arranged," observed Francis. "I wonder what the rest of us will do? I should like just to farm for Missabella, and help raise the dairy cattle."

"And Martha and me will be the cooks," said Marianne positively.

"And dairy-maids," added her twin. "We don't want to leave the place, not ever. Nor does Gavin. He says he's going to build a proper house for us all, one day."

"He says I'm to quarry the stone for it," chimed in Luke. "But that sounds like too much hard work. I'd rather go off and look for gold. Mr. Rose says there could be gold out west."

"Paul wants to be an explorer, so he can join you," Francis suggested. "Only I'm certain Paul will change his mind ten times before he grows up."

"That leaves Sally-Lou—and Missabella will want her to stay at home and be a lady," said Cassie.

"What about Robin?" asked Luke.

Cassie glanced around to see Robin plodding through

the sand with the faithful Cammy.

"He'll just go on being Robin," she said.

The older children were all silent for a little, remembering the morning the mists had closed upon Robin for what had seemed the last time. Now the long crescent of beach was as clean and bright as pearl-shell; then, Francis recollected, it had been grey and damp and hung about with shreds of fog.

"We couldn't see as far as the next point," he said. "But we knew this was the only way they could have gone. The tide had turned, and we could find the footprints in the wet sand. Robin must have walked part of the way, because sometimes there were two sets of prints."

"How frightened he must have been!" said Cassie with a shudder. "Being dragged off to nowhere by the very person he was so scared of!"

He was frightened still, especially in the night when he seemed to hear his father's voice. Gavin and Francis would wake and comfort him, and tell him again and again that his father would not return, but they did not know how much he understood. Missabella said that in time Robin would come to laugh and play and speak a little as he used to—in the meantime, his best medicine was the quiet and undemanding company of Cammy, who was by now so completely accepted as part of the group that the manner of his coming had been quite forgotten.

Cassie dropped back presently to join Eben, who was bringing up the rear in order to keep an eye on all members of the party.

"It was about here that Harry and the others caught sight of Gracechurch," she told him, for Eben and Luke had not returned to the camp till the afternoon of that eventful day.

"He was just climbing round the table-top rock. It's a queer shape, isn't it? I wonder what made it like that."

"They do say this is a very old country," said Eben. "I suppose the sea has had time to carve the land about a bit."

"It's not pretty and neat like our English fields and woods," said Cassie, studying the massed green of the bush bursting from the confines of the shore. "But I like it. It's so big and wild that it makes one feel really free."

She glanced up at Eben apologetically when she realized what she had said; however, he merely smiled a little.

"I don't think Gracechurch would have felt like that."

"He didn't deserve to," said Cassie promptly. "It's not as if he was just a little bit bad—he was *wicked.*"

"So wicked that you're not sorry about what happened to him?" Eben asked curiously.

Cassie hesitated, trying to arrive at the truth about her feelings. With Eben, there was never any need to pretend.

"I suppose I am sorry, in a way," she said at last. "I'm glad I wasn't there at the end, like poor Francis."

Eben saw fit to change the subject.

"While we were staying at Mr. Rose's place, I asked a few questions about how to get my pardon. It seems that in a year or two Mr. Rose and Miss Braithwaite might speak for me, and if I'm lucky I'll go free."

It was only to Cassie that he ever mentioned his hopes and plans, and by an unspoken agreement, they respected each other's confidence. Cassie knew how much this anticipated pardon meant to him, for while his position at Mount St. Matthew had developed into that of trusted and valued servant, to outsiders it still had the old stigma attached.

"Then you might go away," protested Cassie. "And we

should have to find someone else. It could never be the same."

"But you could be grown by that time, and away from home yourself. Whatever happens, things won't stay the same."

"I know," said Cassie, with a sigh. "I so often want to be grown-up, and allowed to do as I please, but another part of me wishes we could all stay together, as we are now. It doesn't matter that we live in palm-tree huts and wear old clothes and catch our own dinner, because we've made ourselves into a real family, and we couldn't have done that in Switherby. I hate to think of our being split up again."

"Not really split up," suggested Eben. "Because you will always have a home to come back to, thanks to your Miss Braithwaite."

"It will be your home, too," said Cassie eagerly. "Even when you're a free man again."

"I hope so," said Eben. And with that brief answer Cassie had to be content.

Soon the party clambered over tumbled rocks to the rough little jetty where Harry's ship had been moored—they knew it had departed some days previously, for Harry himself had come to say good-bye. Missabella had served him tea in the very precious best china cup, part of the set which she had cherished since leaving the vicarage, and although Harry had been in mortal dread of breaking it, he had recognized this as a special honor. Missabella could think of no other way of showing her deep gratitude for what Harry and his friends had done.

"I wish we could all go to Sydney for Harry's wedding," said Selina, who still longed occasionally for an opportunity to dress up. "Sally-Lou could wear her flower-girl's frock again, and I could make myself a new bonnet."

"It won't be a grand wedding at all," said Francis. "It will just happen whenever Harry gets back to Sydney with the timber. Look—from here you can see the water rising from the blowhole."

Beyond a barrier of grey rock, where the blue sky seemed without a vestige of cloud, a sudden white pillar-like shape was thrust upwards, to subside gradually in trails of spray. Where the children stood, at the edge of the sheltered little bay, no sound reached them save the calling of the imperturbable gulls.

"How often does it blow?" Cassie asked, fascinated by the sight.

"It depends on winds and tides, Harry said. When I saw it first, it came up every few minutes, much higher than that, too."

And Francis, abruptly turning his back on the view of the water-spout, suggested that they all have lunch.

"We mustn't take Robin or the twins up there," he whispered to Cassie during the meal. "Especially Robin—he would remember it at once."

But if Robin had felt any uneasiness at this return to Kiarmi, he was not showing it. The picnic lunch had too many attractions, both for himself and Cammy. Missabella had plundered her closely-guarded store of sugar and flour and dried fruits in order to make a birthday cake, and after the scones and cheese and slabs of salted meat had all disappeared, Eben produced the surprise delicacy from his bag. Selina's name had been picked out on the top in sultanas, accompanied by one plump raisin for each of her twelve years, and if the shape of the cake was somewhat irregular —baking on an outdoor fire-place being a decidedly chancy business—no one noticed, because it was tied round with one of Sally-Lou's best pink hair-ribbons.

"It's beautiful!" exclaimed Selina, her blue eyes lighting up with surprised delight. "Do you know, I have never had a cake for my birthday before!"

Cammy, who had not in his brief lifetime tasted cake of any kind, took his share eagerly, not even bothering to finish his *goanna* first. He was deciding that at least some of the white folk's food was palatable, after all.

"We shall take the rest back to Missabella and Gavin," Selina said, carefully re-tying the ribbon round the remains.

"Martha and I helped to make it," said Marianne proudly. "We were the only ones who knew the secret. Missabella said we could make another for our own birthday, only we don't know when it is."

"You're lucky, then," said Cassie promptly. "Because you can choose any day you want, and pick the very best weather."

Lunch over, the smaller children began hunting for shells or exploring the rock-pools, and the twins and Selina volunteered to look after them. Thus only Francis and Cassie, Luke and Eben set out over the headland towards the blow-hole.

"Cammy wouldn't come near it," said Francis. "When we followed Gracechurch as far as this, Cammy just sat down on the beach and refused to move. I expect the black people have their own stories about such a place."

The climb to the point was fairly easy and open, and Cassie looked around her in perplexity.

"Why did Gracechurch come this way? Wouldn't it have been more sensible to have kept away from the rocks?"

Francis looked back at the low bushy-browed hills

clustered along the shore.

"I don't know, but it was so foggy here that you couldn't see far inland. He must have thought he was just crossing another headland, and, anyway, he couldn't have been feeling very sensible by then. He knew he was being followed, I think."

They came to a ledge which dropped away to an unexpected hollow. Beyond it, the ancient piles of rock, strangely crisscrossed with lines made by countless centuries of wind and weather, rose again towards the sea. It was down in the hollow that the deep cleft opened, giving the restless sea an outlet from the cave below. Cassie could hear the invisible waves booming and raging in their rock prison, seeking to find that one narrow chimney above them. As she watched, a tower of spray rose far over her head and sank down with a prolonged pattering.

On a clear benevolent day, in early afternoon, it was still a sinister and threatening place—so much so that even fearless Cassie instinctively drew back. Yet her active imagination made her see it as it must have been on that morning of cold mist and heavy sea, and bade her behold, too, the figures of Gracechurch and his son balanced on the very edge of the dark fissure.

"However did you get Robin?" she asked. "Did Gracechurch let him go?"

Francis moved away and gazed south over soothing creamy sand.

"He had to. He suddenly saw where he was, and he let go Robin's arm. He might even have pushed him away. It all happened so quickly, and Harry was in front of me, shouting something at Gracechurch. I didn't see him after that."

By common consent they all walked towards the land,

with their gaze on the distant dark-blue line of the mountains.

"Whatever happened to Gracechurch, he won't trouble us any more," Eben said. "If he did get away, he would keep on going south."

The water-spout reared up triumphantly, but nobody turned to look. Even the inquisitive Luke had seen enough. Cassie tucked her hand under her brother's arm.

"I'm sorry I made you come," she said. "I didn't know it would be so terrible."

"It's all right," said Francis. "I shall forget about it soon. Spring is not far off, and there will be so many things to do—digging and planting, and Gavin is going to make a hen-house. Then there will be another cow—"

He fell to musing on the prospect of these delights. Cassie left him and started down the broad salt-smelling gradient that led to the harbor.

"It's too good to waste," she said exultantly. "I simply *have* to run!"

Away she raced, tangled hair flying and black-clad ankles unashamedly showing. Luke followed, then Francis, who for the moment let slip the burden of adult cares he had chosen to shoulder. Finally Eben ran too, ran for the first time since his boyhood, and as he went he looked up towards the great open limitless sky, and smiled.

About the Author

Eleanor Spence, born in 1928 in Sydney, New South Wales, is a distinguished writer from Australia. She helped create a literature for children with settings and interest that are authentically Australian. Her fine characterizations, touches of humor, and insight into youth give Mrs. Spence's novels appeal far beyond her own land. She is the author of twenty published books.

Speaking of her childhood days she recalls, in *Something About the Author*, "I *did* set out to be a writer. As a nine-year-old, I scribbled away at my own stories…I loved to read and write about families and I was especially fascinated by orphans. I yearned to adopt neglected infants, [but] had to settle for adopting stray kittens or turning my assortment of dolls into orphanage-waifs." It is clear that the young Eleanor's fondness for orphans worked itself, later on, into the plot of *The Switherby Pilgrims*.

It was while employed in a children's library as a young woman that Eleanor Spence thought she might write, specifically, for children. As it turned out, almost all the author's books follow her natural bent for an audience of *older* children and youth. Over the years she has often presented the circumstance of the young person who in some way is an outsider in his social setting. These circumstances become the springboard for struggle and growth in self-understanding and self-worth. Mrs. Spence notes, "Twice [I have] used handicapped children as central characters—a deaf boy in *The Nothing Place* and an autistic boy in *The October Child*." The situation of autistic children has been a matter of more than casual interest to the author, who has been involved longtime in The Autistic Children's Association.

In the course of her life and writing career, there were times when Eleanor Spence became keenly interested in aspects of Australian history. The character of Missabella, in *The Switherby Pilgrims*, is an echo (although entirely fictional) of the fascinating pioneer, Mrs. Caroline Chisholm, an outstanding woman of the nineteenth century who made provision for young immigrant women in Australia. The effort of the "pilgrims" to establish a new home in the rawness of a strange and difficult land, is one of Mrs. Spence's salutes to the early settlers. In *Jamberoo Road*, the sequel to *The Switherby Pilgrims*, we follow the lives of the Switherby characters as they make a way for themselves in early-day Australia.

Eleanor Spence is perhaps best known in Australian children's literature for her focus on family life. Undoubtedly, her own marriage and raising of three children provided an authentic backdrop for her stories, as did her life-long residence in New South Wales, Australia, the setting for almost all of her books. She says, "I believe the young still find much joy in reading. And writers...still find much joy in writing." This happy combination may be affirmed once more as the work of Eleanor Spence is offered afresh to a new generation of readers.

LIVING HISTORY LIBRARY

The Living History Library is a collection of works for children published by Bethlehem Books, comprising quality reprints of historical fiction and non-fiction, including biography. These books are chosen for their craftsmanship and for the intelligent insight they provide into the present, in light of events and personalities of the past.

TITLES IN THIS SERIES

Archimedes and the Door of Science, by Jeanne Bendick
Augustine Came to Kent, by Barbara Willard
Beorn the Proud, by Madeleine Polland
Beowulf the Warrior, by Ian Serraillier
Big John's Secret, by Eleanore M. Jewett
Enemy Brothers, by Constance Savery
Galen and the Gateway to Medicine, by Jeanne Bendick
God King, by Joanne Williamson
The Hidden Treasure of Glaston, by Eleanore M. Jewett
Hittite Warrior, by Joanne Williamson
If All the Swords in England, by Barbara Willard
Madeleine Takes Command, by Ethel C. Brill
Nacar, the White Deer, by Elizabeth Borton de Treviño
The Mystery of the Periodic Table, by Benjamin D. Wiker
The Reb and the Redcoats, by Constance Savery
Red Hugh, Prince of Donegal, by Robert T. Reilly
The Small War of Sergeant Donkey, by Maureen Daly
Shadow Hawk, by Andre Norton
Son of Charlemagne, by Barbara Willard
Sun Slower, Sun Faster, by Meriol Trevor

continued on next page

The Switherby Pilgrims, by Eleanor Spence
Victory on the Walls, by Frieda C. Hyman
The Winged Watchman, by Hilda van Stockum